Copyright

Lee Wilson

SpeakingSatan

Speakingsatan@gmail.com

R1.3

Thank you, Richard, Barbara, and Julie.
Without you, this may have been a different tale

I have been helped by more people than I could name.
Thank you, everyone.

For my girls as always.

The front cover was designed by Mike Jay Morgan (@LayeredStrange)

# Prologue

There are many worlds out there.

*Wilp - A moment that cannot be changed. Destiny, fate, or wilp.*

We are safe, for now, as we approach the small seaside town of
Burnham on Sea. We could be riding the crest of a wave and looking at the town from the sea as the tide rolls in, but we are not. We are gliding on the wings of a bird, a dove, crow, or maybe a seagull. It doesn't matter; we just watch as the town wakes in the morning. The sunlight bounces from the rooftops as we watch through the eyes of the bird. It blinds our view as it reflects from windows and steel piping. The town is sleepy, but soon it will be the start of something.

We are following the path of *wilp* and letting the bird have control. It can be nice to have control taken from you, I think, to know that sometimes your destiny is not in your own hands. *Wilp* is bigger than any of the things in this world. Even the Heavenly and Hellish creatures will bow to *wilp*. To just go where the wind takes you, we have been taken to a rooftop. We shall wait as it looks for food. Our journey is not yet complete. I would like to point out a curiosity before we get on with the narrative, let's take our time to enjoy the freedom of chance.

Many things have happened on this spot. Love has been discovered, and love has been lost. We are sitting above a pub. Friendships have been made here, and many bones were broken. Across the road, there used to be a train station, long gone now and replaced with a supermarket and car park. This is just an ordinary town. Some months ago, a girl was kidnapped from here. Taken in the night, and not a living soul witnessed it happening.

The girl who was kidnapped was a drifter. Homeless and drifting from place to place. She happened upon this town quite by chance, and any other night she would have been safe. But not, the night in question. She walked the streets cold and alone. As she had been for much of her adult life. Surfing from sofa to sofa at times, but never for long. She was a loner and a drifter. The streets had hardened her in some ways, life and relationships in others. She was still young though, she still had time. She had her looks, her brains, and like many, her dreams. Tonight was different; tonight felt unnatural. Something was wrong. Feeling unsafe was not unusual; she had grown used to that feeling.
Something was clawing at the back of her mind, trying to find its way in.

She looked back over her shoulder and saw nothing. Just stealing a quick glance at the empty street. She appeared to be alone. She had learnt to trust her senses; she'd had to be street smart; she'd had to be aware. She checked once more over her shoulder before continuing. She tapped the small three-inch bar that she held in her hand with her thumb. This was the seafront of a small town. It may have been late summer, but It should not have been this quiet. She looked up and down the street, and it was empty, not a soul in sight. No cars for anyone to hide behind, no dark alleys for someone to jump from. She should have felt safe, *and yet*, she still felt that something was wrong. She felt that she was being watched. Observed and, dare she think it? Hunted!

A car rounds the corner, and her heartbeat quickens. The drip drip drip of a tap starts to loosen as the washer fails at record speed. Drip drip drip, beat beat beat becoming dripdripdrip. She walks faster, not too fast, but also not too slow. Just a quickening of pace that is designed not to show fear. The car is approaching now, and it is slowing. Matching her pace and following just behind. She grasps the bar she holds in her hand. Clenching her fist around it, it won't be without a fight if she is going down. The car crawls as she walks, and she resists the urge to turn and look. She pushes the thought of running from her mind. If it is nothing, she will look a fool. If it is something, she wants them to make the first move. This tactic has seen her well in the past. "Hello dear, would you like a cup of tea", an elderly ladies voice asked. She stopped on the corner of the road. A mild hesitation, It's then that it happens.

The street falls dark, all the streetlights switching off at once. A power cut? She would never know. The woman in the car stared at her through the window without saying a word. Then the second bout of darkness hit, and this time it was from behind. She fell forward but was grabbed at the last moment. Her assailant had snuck up on her as she stopped at the corner. The car and streetlights taking all of her attention from her. The woman in the car sat, saying or doing nothing. The man who had hit her with a club held her easily. She was slight and light through years of undereating and the never-ending wandering. He quickly dragged her to the boot of the car. The boot was popped, and the girl deposited within. Thrown like an unwanted sack of kittens. The man got into the car without saying a word, and the car drove off, the streetlights relighting one by one as it did so.

Away we go, back to the skies on our tour. That was the last anyone ever saw of the girl. Kidnapped and taken, never to be seen again. It is funny how when you let it *wilp* takes you to places of importance. If we look down, we can see the streets below, still empty at the moment, but they will be bustling with people soon enough. People going about their day to day lives. The seafront road runs parallel to the high street, with roads intersecting to connect the two. The round catholic church sits in the distance, small and thrifty. The very opposite of the COE one that sits at the other end of the town.

Gliding past M&S as we make our way towards our destination. A road that is more of a street but still called a lane. A place where stories begin and end. A resting place waiting to awaken. A house sits at the end of the lane. It is the house where our wandering girl met her end. The end of her story, and yet, the beginning of ours.

# Egress

Daniel James is a paranormal researcher; it was something he had done since his twenties. Nearly two decades in the business, and still, he had not, until this point, found any actual proof. He had walked away for a period five years earlier, not because he no longer believed. Many who worked in the trade become so disillusioned that they give it up. The optimism of youth told them that they would be the one; they'd be the one who proved it all. Exposing the ghosts and goblins, proving life after death. Maybe even a meet and greet with Lilith and Satan. Then the realisation came in mid-life that you'll not prove it, and perhaps it did not actually exist. Still, he was dragged back to the trade. Maybe all that was left at the end of it all was to be worm food. If that were the case, then why not go out hunting for the truth and fighting?

It was not the notoriety that had seduced him. It was not the idea of fame - r*elative though it may have been* - it was the question. It was the idea of knowing that something else was out there. To actually know beyond any doubt. The thought of saying, definitively, that there was something after death and here is the proof. That was what had driven him; that was what had pushed him forwards for all these years. *So why did he stop?* What had made him take a break when he hit his late-thirties? Well, he had found what he was looking for, and it had terrified him. It had shaken him to his very core, screamed "*Why hello there*" into his face and then laughed as he had run from it.

## *2015*

Daniel sat waiting in his car, flicking through the latest discoveries on his phone. It was his daily ritual. He had to know this stuff. He would check for any new ideas, new tricks that could be used to con the gullible into parting with their money in exchange for a *visit* with the deceased. The trick levitating tables, the smoke machines and mirrors used to create effects. The practice was always trying to find new ways to con the naive, so he also had to continually read, learn, and modernise his methods. Trying to keep one step ahead, or at worse to be level pegging. Answering a question with "I do not know how they did it" would lead to the death-knell in his profession.

This job was different. This one would be easy. A haunted house,
*haunted* being a term he had always used loosely.

Two thoughts would traverse his mind when a h*aunted house* case file dropped on his desk. Firstly, the obvious one, *ha this would be easy*. Dripping pipes, wind seeping through cracks in window frames, creaking floorboards and all other non-supernatural events. What a load of bollocks. Secondly, a long, drawn-out moan of boring would echo the darkest corners of his mind.

Bouncing from side to side and up and down as his eyes rolled back in his head.

He would have found more excitement at a political discussion group.

The most intriguing investigation that Daniel had been involved with was the Burke house. *Once again*, it had not been supernatural, but at least it had been *different*. It had been interesting. It had started with a noise that would be heard occasionally in one wall. It would be heard primarily at night, but not only at night. It was never clear enough to precisely determine what was being said. Never quite sure if anything really was being said, if it was even a voice at all. It was random, intermittent static, and beholden to whatever *power* that was causing it. The mind has a way of seeing patterns in things, faces in objects and speech in noises.

Maybe it was something, maybe it was nothing, but maybe, just maybe, it was everything! Without fail, it would reoccur. Sometimes days would pass and sometimes weeks, but it had always come back. Finally, Daniel came across the case file and took it up. It had been floating in and around the Institute's offices for a while, waiting to be investigated. Ninety minutes later, and with the help of a smartphone, the issue had been resolved. The most supernatural element in the case? How the batteries had lasted so long? The best two quid he had ever spent was on the *Architecture of Radio* app. It was capable of detecting radio signals, and it gave you a visual reference. Red for a weak signal, orange for medium and green for strong. It was mainly used for séances, but it had other uses too.

Before Daniel had taken the case, the usual cranks had been, saying that it was most definitely a sign of some otherworldly presence. Within two hours *total*, it was all over. A sheet of plasterboard had been cut from the wall and the culprit identified. A previous tenant or owner had lost a baby monitor down inside the wall. It had been chewed by a rodent, and by pure chance, had shorted and would intermittently turn itself on. Something purely natural that had given the impression of the *supernatural*. It had picked up a signal from somewhere nearby; where? It held no real relevance as cross chat on these things was not an uncommon occurrence. It could have been any of the houses nearby, or it may have just been electrical cracking and hissing. The monitor had been removed, the wall was patched back up, and the problem was resolved. One more being filed into the depths of his mind and office filing cabinet. Mission accomplished, case closed and *thank you for tuning in. Join us next time on tales of the disappointing...*

As Daniel sat in his car, he looked at the house and its grounds. Something niggled at him. Buzzing around his mind like a fly caught in a net curtain. A thought floated up from the depths but sunk back underwater the second he tried to seize hold. Something was not right, and the fact that he could not put his finger upon it unnerved him. A shiver swept its way down his spine. People had often mistaken his ability to see things that others missed for a sixth sense; it was nothing of the sort. All he had is the ability to notice things, nothing more and nothing less. He would see things that others would overlook. Linking two things and coming up with a solution. He'd not realised it at the time, but the baby monitor had been his mind doing just that. A friend had bought the same monitor a decade earlier and experienced a similar problem with the interference. It was the static in the background that had set his mind searching for the link, not the noise it had picked up but the static. There was a familiarity, the connection, and it would take some weeks before it had finally clicked and he had remembered.

Daniel sat and tapped his fingers upon the steering wheel, something felt wrong here, and he couldn't quite work out what it was. Annoyed with himself, he opened the car door, stepped out and slammed it shut. The windows in the old wreck rattled like panes in an old greenhouse as he did so. The car was a mess, but it was his mess. It worked and did what he wanted, besides he thought. Who was going to nick his old clapped out 2CV?

Daniel stood and looked down the road at the closed gates. He'd had to park away from the house as the driveway was gated and bolted. The short driveway led to the detached house with a road crossing just before the gates. The place he had been sent to see stood alone in the distance. The upper floor windows looked like sets of drooping eyes watching him. The trees that led up either side of the driveway were neatly pruned, clipped and in places pinned back. The drive itself was clear of leaves and other rubbish that he would have expected this time of year. Then it hit him. The mental block crumbled, allowing him to see; that was it, that was what had been wrong. Once he had looked at it, it was so obvious, but it had taken him longer than he would usually have expected. Longer than he'd have liked. The house had been empty for years; it had nobody to maintain it. The family had once tried, but nobody would stay for long. In the end, falling like dominos, the family line was broken and lost. The house and grounds were all that remained. Its current owners are seemingly unknown, the house managed by a group of solicitors.

*So who had been maintaining the trees?*

It couldn't have been squatters or the homeless, could it? Garden maintenance was not something they were known for as far as he knew. Besides, had they taken over, then being spotted by a passer-by would have been the last thing they'd wanted. *Hi everyone, we're just squatting here, so just ignore us.* Daniel

Checked his pocket for his tools and a padlock, and he then headed toward the gate. He reached the road that intersects, looked both ways and crossed. He looked at the entrance; it was locked and secured just as it should have been. The large metal gate was spattered with rust spots giving it an orange tinge far more in keeping with the season.

Daniel pulled the lock picking set from his pocket, plucking between the picks and pins. He slid the guide into the bottom of the padlock and slipped a pin in beside it. Closing his eyes and imagining the lock and the pins the way that he had trained himself. Visualising the lock's inside as he moved the pin, *click*. The lock was rusted, but it fell open with ease. Permission had been granted from the solicitors that dealt with the estate, so he had no need to be worried about being discovered. Nobody knew what had happened to the original keys; it had been so long since the house had been inhabited. He could have employed a locksmith, but he liked to work alone. Why hire someone to do a job that he could do himself? The lock was removed and discarded onto the ground. He took the fresh one from his pocket and unlocked it as he opened the gate. The metal creaked with age as he pushed it. He walked through the small gap and pushed the gate closed. He slipped the new lock into place, pocketed the key and then left the lock open and hanging on the latch.

Daniel stood for a moment alone and in silence. It was just the way that he liked things to be. As he walked the drive, he admired the trees and the pristine condition they were in. The leaves were still green when they should have been tinting to autumn orange. He shook his head; how did he miss that? It all seemed so obvious now. He noticed that the house seemed to be in good condition as well. The house was half brickwork and half wood. The bottom brickwork he would have expected to see was chipped and discoloured after all this time. The top should have been peeling with paint flecks falling away to reveal rotting wood below. Neither thing had happened. The upstairs had the look of almost being freshly painted. The bricks downstairs glowed with a pale red colour, extruding life and freshness.

Something was not as it would seem. Daniel considered heading back to the car and searching the boot for the jack handle or lug wrench but decided against it. So what if a few homeless people were living here? They had looked after the place and may need help, not violence and threats. *Why hello there. I mean no harm. Oh, sorry, ignore this big metal tyre iron. I'm just happy to see you. I always come carrying metal.* He looked at the steps that led to the front door, expecting to see some dereliction, a sign of age and a lack of maintenance. They appeared as fresh and new as they would have been on the day that they were built. He placed his foot on one and pushed hard; he did not want to be deceived. It did not budge. It was still as strong as it had ever been. He took a step and made his way to the front door. The steps were soundless, with not a creak or wheeze to be heard.

The doors stood before Daniel at an imposing eight feet. They were made of oak and gigantic; they appeared to open centrally. Two doors that alone were huge and no doubt heavier than most standard household doors. Houses that were built with height, space, and grounds, a long-forgotten commodity. He turned to take another look around the front garden; they'd fit ten homes here in today's world, he supposed to himself. The grass was neatly trimmed and the flower beds, though empty, were free from weeds. Just the brown soil ready for those seeds to be sown in the spring. Were things better in the past, or was it just a fondness for an imagined world that did not really exist? Maybe a little of both, he decided.

Daniel reached into his pocket for the lock picking set once more but then decided against it. If someone was living here, he does not want to spook them; *I come in peace*. Reaching up and knocking on the door, he then listened but heard nothing. He then lifted the large metal knocker and dropped it; it boomed through the wood as he let it go. He expected to hear a shuffling of feet, the sounds of movement, something, anything, yet he still heard nothing. Not a whisper or scratch of movement from inside the house. He placed his hand upon the door handle. It was a solid brass handle that matched the knocker, and it felt unexpectedly warm. It was like somebody had stood holding it for a period just before he had arrived. He twisted it, and the handle moved smoothly and turned with no resistance. The place was unlocked, and the door swung open. With the door now open, he stepped inside. "Hello", Daniel called out, "I come in peace. I mean you no harm". As soon as he stepped inside, the temperature change was apparent, not colder as he would have expected in a traditional *haunting*, but warmer. A handful of degrees, but it was a noticeable difference. He ran his hand along the top of the hallway radiator. It was stone cold. He lifted his hand, looked at it, and saw not a speck of dust. He looked around the hallway, and everything is immaculate. He had expected to see dust covers over any items still remaining, but this looked like the house had just been tidied, awaiting his arrival.

Daniels mind ticked over, joining the dots, adding it all together, trying to find a logical conclusion. He stood for a moment thinking and then kneeled with his right knee on the ground. *There it is*, he thought, and then he placed his hand down on the floor just to double-check. The mystery of the cleanliness could come later; for now, he had found the heat source. Heat rises, and it was coming from below. He grabbed his phone from his pocket and looked at the plans he had for the house. Zooming in and out, he searched the pictures for a basement or utility room that was below. *The master staircase's left-hand side, into, and through, the kitchen and then to the left.* Pushing the phone back into his pocket, he ventured forwards. The floorboards finally creaked under his weight as he made his way to the kitchen.

The kitchen was as spotless and tidy as the hallway. The house's contents should have been looted or rotted and consumed by time and neglect. But, instead, it looked like someone had loved and cared for it all. Daniel shook his head.

*This wasn't right; something was wrong. This wasn't part of the script. It was meant to be windy windows, creaky floorboards, and rattling pipes. This was wrong.*

Daniel felt an urge to turn and leave rush through him. He suppressed it, pushing it to the back of his mind. He had never been a coward; he would not have allowed himself to be. You couldn't be in his line of work! Monsters under the bed, creepy crawling shadows from the closet, those were all bollocks, inventions of an overactive imagination. *Now those were part of a script.* The scariest thing in the world was your imagination, and once you let it run riot and take over, you leave yourself wide open.

*Here be nightmares, do not enter if you scare easily.*

Daniel placed his hand on the door to the basement and pushed it open. The door flew open with ease, its hinges well maintained and loose-fitting in the frame. He looked down the wooden stairs into the blackness below. There was a curiosity here, he noted. A trick of the light that caused a strange effect. The basement seemed to suck the light from the kitchen. Light reached the frame of the basement door and then went no further. Daniel moved his hand between the basement and the kitchen. Well lit in the kitchen, shadowed the second he went beyond the doorframe. *Weird.* He flicked the light switch for the basement, and of course, there was no power. Daniel tapped the torch app on his phone and lit the stairway. *Be prepared* as his Scoutmaster had always said to him. He tested the steps as he had done outside, secure and stable, he started his descent. One step, then two, then three, one hand gripped the bannister, the other held the phone and lit the way. The light from the phone flickered, and then suddenly, the phone went utterly blank. The steps beneath his feet gave. They didn't just give from age or structural weakness. There was no cracking and flexing of the wood. One moment they were there. The next, they were gone along with the bannister, and he found himself falling into the darkness below. He was being swallowed just as the light had been from the kitchen.

Daniel lay on the floor; his eyes were closed. He had closed them as he fell. *What the fuck just happened?* he thought. His foot was half step, and even had one step given out, he would have been able to balance his weight on the other. He had learnt before to take one step with one foot. Slow and steady wins the race. It was as if they had just vanished. He'd got lucky, the fall had not been that far, and as it was straight down, he had landed feet first. It could have been much worse. Just as he was about to reopen his eyes, he heard it, a noise, the slightest movement in the dark. Something skittering in the blackness, coming from the corner of the room. Something or someone was in the room with him. He kept quiet. Subconsciously he held his breath, eyes closed and mentally glued shut. He tried to listen and hoped to go unnoticed. There was just something wrong about this; a feeling swam in his stomach. The ruffling stopped, and all was still. He took a peek, just a little slide of an eyelid. Enough to see, but - *hopefully* - not enough to be seen. The room was now light, an unnatural light that engulfed every angle. Listening once more, trying to hear anything out of the ordinary. The room had fallen silent. He opened his eyes fully and looked around the room.

The room was empty, a square box room with just a well at its centre. No windows, no doors, no light fittings to be seen and nothing - *that Daniel could see* - skittering around in the corners. He looked up, the door was still there, but it was too high to reach. The stairs were gone, vanished into nothing.

Vanished from sight as if they had never been. He looked around the room. There must be another exit somewhere. There did not seem to be any source for the light. The beams of wood that made the floor of the room above let a little peek through but were nowhere near enough to light this whole basement. Checking from beam to beam, he saw nothing that could answer the question of the lights source. Tentatively he walked to the corners of the room, checking before every step for something lurking. Something that could somehow loiter in this strange brightness, he found nothing. Just the four corners, the four walls and the well in the centre. Anger overtook fear, and he was suddenly annoyed; *this must be someone's idea of a practical joke*. The how's and why's never crossed his usually logical mind. Anger had suffocating logic and reason with a mental pillow. "Okay, you got me!" He shouted out to nobody but the room. Following up by muttering "You fuckers" under his breath. He stood and waited. Hope rather than an expectation that the door would fly open and some of his younger, more exuberant colleagues would be there laughing at him. He stood there a little longer than was needed, deep in thought. His imagination then took over; what if this was not a prank? What if this *really was* something else?

Daniel moved closer to the well; it was all that he had left to investigate. He was aware that his mind decided to first check the things that he could already see. He knew that looking down the well was looking into the unknown, gazing into the mouth of madness. When you look into madness, madness looks right back at you with a smile. It was, though, his only choice. He took a long deep breath and approached the centre of the room.

On the one hand, he was glad to be alone so nobody could see how shaken he was. On the other? He'd rather have had company. He placed his hands on the stones around the well and could feel the heat rising from the shaft. *Well, I found the heat source*. He almost had to dare himself to lean over the well, *double dare*. A blast of hot air hit his face as he looked over, like being slapped by an angry girlfriend. It forced him to turn and look away. He held his hand out into the room, testing the temperature. It was warm but not hot; a pleasant spring day. He dangled his hand over the well and felt the warm, heated air. The closer to the centre, the warmer it got, too hot to touch at threequarters of the way. Not quite the bowels of Hell on the hottest day of the year, but close enough. He withdrew his arm, his hand shivered at the sudden temperature change. Suddenly he felt something under his foot, something different, something that wasn't there before. Couldn't have been there before.
He took a step backwards.

The ground beneath Daniel's feet was just soil. Compacted by years of use, but soil nonetheless. The wooden framework of the house was built up around the soft under-base. The man who builds his house on the sand had obviously not applied in this case. Poking up through the earth was a small, ivory-coloured, tiny triangle-shaped object. A small pea of a strange rock budding up through the ground. It cannot have been there before; he would have felt it as he stood next to the well. It did nothing as he looked at it, just there where it was not before, sprouted from nothing. He moved his foot towards it, his mind telling him not to touch it with his bare skin, or in this case, leather shoe. Something warned him against that, just a feeling. He pushed the rubble slightly with the end of his shoe; as he did so, the object moved, a small creamcoloured stone driving up through the dirt. He thought it could be his mind playing tricks at first, but then it moved again. It twitched slightly, wiggling like a worm as it appeared, making its way to the surface. It was slow at first, fascinatingly sluggish, and he was mesmerised by it until he realised what it was. It was the notch three-quarters of an inch down that gave it away. The object shifted through, becoming taller. Some kind of strange albino plant growing in real-time. The join, though, he knew then it was a skeletal hand pushing through. Only one finger now, but it was moving faster.

# The Sacrifice

Daniel looked around the room once again, looking for an escape. He scanned the four walls, he jumped for the door. Hoping that it could be reached, *knowing* that it was far too high. He slumped into a corner of the room. Not wanting to look, he could hear the noise of it as it burrowed free. What was once slow was now moving at speed. The scraping, scratching and shifting of the mud seemed to be amplified in his ears. Dirt being pushed to one side by an ever-larger set of bones returning to the surface. He pushed his back against the wall, turning as he did to face this demon. He heard a mocking voice in his head that rebounded at speed in the cavities of his brain; it hopped and bounced from side to side. It made it feel like his head was going to explode.

*Well, you wanted proof, so come now, come and see it.*

Daniel scuttled up in the corner of the room into a foetal position. Knees high up around his neck. He slid himself to the back wall feeling his spine pushing against the cool, cold, rugged brickwork. Imagining that the wall would take more of him, maybe absorb him fully and take him from this nightmare. His feet dug into the ground, causing the dirt and rubble to move away and gave him more leverage to push against the wall. The sound of his scraping was eerily familiar to the noise the bones had made as they had broken free. Now that he had looked, he could not look away. The skeleton was halfway out, digging itself free. The fingers dug and stabbed into the ground like a garden fork as it pulled itself from its grave. Its mouth fell open, and it looked at Daniel. *Is it trying to speak*? No noise escaped the hollow of the mouth. It just continued its release as Daniel cowered in the corner. It moved faster now that the skeleton was at its knees. It pulled itself from the empty makeshift grave that it had once inhabited. It was now free; the mouth still moved as if trying to communicate, trying to voice some unspeakable evil. The bones chittered and chattered as it moved, but the mouth was silent. Then it was entirely out, on all fours, and it looked at Daniel. The black, dark, empty, bowled sockets seemed to stare right through him. Staring into the nothingness that was maybe not for human eyes. The arms clicked, turned ninety degrees, bending at angles that would be unnatural for any human body. The whole creature lurched over sideways in one quick bony action. It was now upside down. The arms now supported the body's front, holding it up. The legs clicked around as the supporting arms had done, lifting the body's rear; it was almost crab-like. The head upside down twisted slowly, clicking and snapping as it did so. Finally, it all stopped, and everything fell quiet for just the briefest of moments.

The crab-like skeleton continued to watch Daniel with its eyeless sockets. It felt like an age of nothing. That moment in between seeing an object and tripping over it. Then the monster lurched forward, and it pinned Daniel against the wall. The bones clacked and rattled back into place as it leant forwards. The skull was an inch from Daniel's face, and he was frozen with fear. He could hear the bones grinding together like rocks. A sweet smell dangled under his nose; something that had maybe once been flesh lingered, teasing him.

Pinned or not, everything about this situation was shouting *run*, but his body just would not respond. Paralysed by fear, crippled by shock, he could only watch and stare like a deer caught in headlights waiting for the oncoming radiator.

    The creature forced its skull against Daniel's. This jammed his head back against the wall, sinking ever harder into the stone. At that moment, images flashed before him. A slideshow of horror in his visual cortex. The images sped up until he could see it all.

    Daniel looked around the room, the vision of three people, two performing a dark ritual. Two dark hooded figures and one dressed in white and bound to a stake in the ground. The stake bound woman was struggling with the ropes that held her. She was dressed in a flimsy nightgown, and with the kindling at her feet, it would not have taken Sherlock Holmes to deduce what was to come.

Daniel started to call out, to shout something, but he found his voice mute. Like screaming for help underwater, his voice was muffled and only heard by himself. He watched in horror as the smaller of the two cloaked figures approached the stake. The woman at the stake pleaded with the approaching figure. "Please, you don't have to do this". Her tear-filled sobs as she spoke came to Daniel as crystal clear as any modern radio broadcast. The other person replied, and this was an older woman. It was someone who sounded quite pleasant and calm. An old Aunt maybe who was pulling a splinter from their niece or nephew. "Now, now dear", she said. "You know I can't do that". The words, as kind as they were, rattled from her mouth like venom from a snake. The lack of empathy and compassion in that voice seemed to suck the tiny hopes from the staked woman. Her head bowed down, and the tears fell from her cheek onto the nightgown.

The hooded woman lit a match and waved it in front of the others face. Torture, toying with her victim. "It will all be over soon dear", she said as coldly as ever as she dropped the match. The match took an age to fall. It fell like the frames in an old movie had slowed. Twisting through the air impossibly held alight until it met the kindling. The flames took hold instantly, and Daniel tried once again to call out. To do anything to save this girl. He watched on paralysed and unable to call for help as the flames jumped from the kindling to the thin fabric of the nightdress. He closed his eyes and tried to block out the screams as the fire raced up her legs. He saw everything projected onto the insides of his eyelids. No accelerant had been used, well none that Daniel had seen, but the body burnt like old newspaper on a bonfire. Flames danced and raced up her legs and body as she screamed a curdled scream of the damned.

Fire danced up the dress and smothered her head. The screams thankfully died a death along with her long flowing hair. Her skin crackled and burnt, allowing the reds and oranges of the season to mix with the charred black flaking tissues. The burnt and blistered tissue fell away, her life still holding on somehow.

*Black cloaks for a black mass in a black basement.*

The fire burnt through the ropes that held her, and as she slouched forwards, the bindings broke, and her body fell to the floor. She put her arms out as she fell and regretted it instantly. The burning skin tore as she moved, and when her hands hit the ground, pain ripped through her body. She tried to scream, but her mouth was filled with only soot, charred lips and pain. Smoke rose from her as she lay on the ground, deserting its host and scurrying away like a naughty toddler, hiding from what it had done.

Daniel watched the two hooded figures. They just stood watching the smouldering body. Daniel could not see it, but smiles formed on their mouths as they watched the sacrifice in pain. If they could have, they would have sucked the fear, pain, and life from her there and then. As if sensing this, the second hooded figure spoke. This time it was a man's voice. "Not today. You know what today is all about", he said. "Go and get it", the man ordered. Daniel was as shocked as he was and as scared as his brain would allow him to still took notes. A man and a woman, he thought, making a mental memory, something to hold on to. The hooded woman followed the instruction and walked to the charred body. She grabbed a hold of the arm. The body groaned as she dragged it towards the centre of the room, towards the well. "Good, now throw her in", the man commanded. Following orders, the body was thrown into the well. It doesn't splash or smash; the drop is soundless, never-ending. The shaft of darkness swallowing the body whole in one large gulp.

"That is it, my dear", the man said to the woman with obvious affection. "Just the two of us left now". The very moment the man finished speaking, the room changed. The atmosphere dropped a dozen degrees in heat, and both the hooded figures started to expel white misty steam each time they let out a breath. Suddenly Daniels inner voice spoke to him, only this time it was different. This time it was female.

*Count darlings, there are four of you.*

Daniel scanned the room as best he could. The two hooded figures, the man and woman, the girl who had been thrown down the well and himself. That made four, but... The man who had been issuing orders suddenly looked up, and Daniel then got a good look at this leader. "Four?" the man said, questioning. He had heard the voice too! He recognised the face straight away from pictures he'd seen at the Institute, Faustus McGovern, but how? The man waved his arms and hands in a circular motion. Chanted in Elden and looked around the room. He had the paranoid look of someone caught in the act. Finally, he settled on the place where Daniel was watching. Faustus looked at Daniel, right at him; Faustus could see him. "Be-gone", he shouted and waved his arm like a magician performing a trick. This time commanding Daniel and only Daniel. The room suddenly became dark, pitch black, and Daniel fell to the ground with a thud; he moaned as he landed and looked to his side. He could see his phone lying on the floor, torchlight still active and shining up, lighting the staircase.

Daniel grabbed his phone from the floor and quickly pointed the light around the room. He didn't want to look, but he had to; he couldn't not. *It was who he was.* The room was empty, nothing to be seen; even the well shaft was now capped. The dust had made itself at home, long settled on the wooden planks that covered it. His heart raced like an out of control locomotive bouncing between sleepers. The house had an aged scent now. The dank, musty smell escaped from every crevice. The smell of age and rot twisted its way up around the hairs in his nose. He moved to the stairs, placing a foot on one and pushing. *A force of habit.* It whined under his weight but felt stable enough. *Fuck it*, he was not staying down here a moment longer. He surged forwards, taking two steps at once and made it safely to the top.

*Rules are made to be broken.*

# Departing Egress

The door was opened in a flash, and Daniel dashed into the kitchen, slamming the door behind. The doorframe rattled and dust and fell to the floor. It danced in the slight breeze that now came through the kitchen. The kitchen, like the basement, was now aged and ragged; dirt and grime covered everything. He ran to the door that led to the hallway, grabbed the handle and slammed against it, *locked*! He used his shoulder and tried to barge the door open; it would not move. It was like the door had been drawn upon a wall, rock-solid. Checking for a lock, he saw nothing, just a handle that would not budge. "Well, you can't go through there yet", a cheerful voice said from behind. He turned instinctively quickly, his nerves were on edge, and he did not want to be blindsided again.

An elderly lady sat at a table in the centre of the kitchen; *neither were there before.* She was pouring two cups of tea from a china teapot, never once taking her eyes from Daniel. Her blouse of white silk swayed slightly in the breeze. She poured the cups of tea, put the teapot down, and then reached into her lap, pulled a pistol, and placed it upon the table. She left her hand resting upon it. "Milk or sugar?" she asked, a smile forming on her lips as she did so. She just ignores the pistol and acts as if it were not there. Daniel knew the voice. He had not seen her face, but he knew the voice. So this was a ghost, he thought. This was an actual haunting. "You were down there", Daniel said and pointed at the door he had just come running through. "And now, I am up here", the woman replied.

"You're Meredith, I take it?" Daniel asked. He stood firm, rooted to the spot, determined to not show any weakness. The woman shook her head as if this was a silly thing to ask. "My dear, I am the housekeeper". She took a sip of her tea, "Why don't you sit down dear, you look like you've had quite the shock". *Her voice was laced with playfulness; she was taunting him.* Daniel stood his ground and said nothing. His mind was racing to explain the illogical with the logical, somehow trying to make two and two add up to four. It failed; he kept rolling five. He knew this woman. This thing that sat before him was real. She was, however a ghost, or something else. "Are you a ghost?" He asked.

"Deary, I am something else. Something different", Meredith replied.

*There must be something that makes sense, something that can explain this,* Daniel thought. He looked at the windows and considered it as a possible escape; if he can't make the front door, desperate measures may be needed. The frames now looked fragile enough to break in a strong wind, never mind a fullygrown man charging them. The rear door was on the other side of the room; he'd never be able to reach it. "Oh, I wouldn't try that", Meredith said knowingly. "I may be old, but I only need one of the six bullets in this pistol". She patted the pistol and then took another sip before continuing. "I only have to make sure you get through that door. I do not have to make sure you do so unharmed. So please, try the window or door. I'd rather enjoy shooting you".

She placed her cup down and put a finger inside the trigger guard. Her grey eyes watched everything. Daniel thought about rushing her; he was sure he could have got to her before she could aim and fire, but could he stop her from firing a wild shot? Of that, he was not so sure. Did it matter? She had him where she wanted him. "So what now?" He asked her, and this time she said nothing; she just sat in silence and watched. "What do you want?" Daniel snapped.

"Want, sweetheart? Want has nothing to do with it".

Daniel could not help thinking of how a predator watched its prey. Meredith finished speaking, and then she started to laugh abruptly, not a laugh that built. This is a burst of full-throttled hysterical laughter from the start. Her head jerked to the side quickly and suddenly and then backwards as she continued to laugh. Her eyes stared at the hanging light above. Daniel started to edge closer to the windows, thinking that he could not be seen as Meredith sat looking at the ceiling. She chortled with laughter; her eyes watched the light as it swung back and forth. She raised the gun and pointed it right at him; she did not look once. Her laughter continued throughout, heckling him. There was a tear as she leant her head back further, the tearing of old fabric or leather. Her lips started to tear along the cheeks as her head flopped backwards, almost coming completely free. A smile all the way back to her ears to match the laugh. It was impossibly hanging by the muscle and skin that remained. The gargling of laughter continued. The head now hanging back, insides exposed, tongue waggled in the air. Opened like a book of gossip with the tongue flopping like a bookmark. Gurgling drowned laughter continued as she got to her feet in one swift movement. Her long brown skirt fell to cover her feet. The table got knocked as she did so, teacups and pot spilt and crashed to the floor. The noise from the shattered china shook Daniel from staring at the woman's head, and he reached, once again, for the door handle.

Daniel did not hold out any hope, but as the woman hobbled towards him, he pushed it, and this time it opened. Meredith staggered forwards, wobbling from side to side with her errant tongue swaying in tune with the insane laughter. He shoved the door open and then crashed it shut as he ran through. He dared not look back. Not even a double dare would have worked this time. The hallway remained quiet. It was as dead as he had expected it to have been when he had first arrived. The remnants of the old furniture scattered around, with dust covering everything like a thick layer of grey sandy paint. He kept his back pressed against the door, and then he heard the single gunshot and, finally, a thud. He thought about peeking, *triple dare ya*, but he did not need to. He knew what had just happened in the kitchen. He knew it as well as he had known the Burke house was not a haunting, and now he only had to face what, if anything, awaited him in the rest of the hallway.

The hallway lay ominously silent, Daniel knew that there must be something up ahead, but he could hear or see nothing. He could have heard a pin drop, a hammer fall, or the sheet of a ghost whispering along the floor. Dust swirled in the air. It danced its dance where it had been disturbed by the opening and closing of long-forgotten doors. He almost tiptoed his way towards the front door to avoid the creaking floorboards as he walked. Those boards that waited, ready to alert the idle dead. Hairs stood on the back of his neck and twitched. Shivering along with the dance of the dust. A Tango of torment. His senses were checking out everything, looking for anything that should not be. He eased closer to the door, one step at a time and alert to everything. He expected something to jump, hop, drop or slop out at any moment and finish him off. He finally made it and grasped the handle tightly; this time, it was cold to the touch. He tried to open it, and for just the briefest moment, he thought it would be locked, but then it opened. Daniel pulled the door fully open and stepped outside; he took in a deep breath of the fresh, clean air. Dust, dirt, mud, skeleton, and Meredith free air. Standing outside the front door, his heartbeat started to slow to a more regular speed.

*What had happened? What had he seen?*

He looked over at the trees; all of them were now overgrown, the driveway mostly covered with grass and moss. The flower beds now crawled with weeds and grass. The grass would be almost to his knees when he walked away from the house. Nature had taken back what was owed, the house and grounds now devolving back to what he had first expected. Daniel moved forward, ready to run for the gate. He was ready to dart when a figure stepped out in front of him. "Going somewhere?" the hooded figure asked him. "Faustus", Daniel growled, the disgust in his voice not disguised in the slightest, "But you can't be. You're dead".

"It is all a matter of perspective. You would say dead, but I would say waiting and learning", Faustus replied. Daniel took a step back towards the doorway as Faustus moved forwards toward the steps. Faustus wore the same cloak that Daniel had seen in his vision; he pulled his hood down to reveal his face as he approached. The face was withered and worn from the years, but there was more than that. With the scarring on his left cheek and the fatigue in his eyes, the man was tired. So, so tired, and the eyes had the look of a man who was doing as he was ordered, not as he wanted. They looked unhappy to be there. They were glazed with the look of someone doing something against their will. A man holding a gun while his partner was held hostage elsewhere. A green with a hint of fear mixed together swam with the dot of a pupil as he watched Daniel.

Daniel lifted his foot slightly and pushed backwards on the door, testing to make sure it was still open, and it was. He'd feared that somehow the door had closed behind him and locked itself as the kitchen door had done. The house itself laughing and playing games with him. "We can go inside if you would like", Faustus said as he looked down at Daniel's foot, "Or, we can talk here". Holding his hands up in front of himself, Faustus tried to give the impression that he was harmless. Daniel wasn't buying it. "Back away", Daniel ordered. He did not expect anything to come from it, but Faustus took a step back and hesitated. "What do you want with me?" Daniel asked with newfound confidence. "You?" Faustus laughed, "Oh, it is not you. You are just", he paused for a moment like he was awaiting instruction or a direction. Maybe just finding the right word or buying himself time. "You are just, shall we say a spark, a means to an end". Faustus stepped forward quickly, one hand out. He grabbed at Daniel. In one quick motion, Daniel pushed the hand away and turned to run back inside the house.

Daniel kicked the door open, and Meredith stood in the doorway, head still half flopped back. Her insane giggling crone-like laughter started again. The bullet had ripped through her lower jaw and destroyed her tongue, splitting it in two. It looked like the split in a serpent tongue; even the parting could not stop the noise that laughed, gargled and hacked from inside her long-dead throat. Daniel looked down and saw the pistol still in her hand. He expected a fight and for her to pull away the moment he reached forward, but she did not. She just stood swaying like an old drunk late at night, oblivious to what was really going on. He pulled the gun away from her with ease, and he then turned it and pointed it at Meredith. He pulled the trigger twice, *bang bang*, but the bullets just sank into her; she just stood as if nothing had happened, just the continuous laughter filling the space between them. Her ample bosom absorbed the bullets. No blood spilt; there only remained small black holes in her blouse as evidence of the violence. Daniel turned, and this time he pointed the gun at Faustus. "Stand back, or I'll shoot", he shouted coldly. Faustus said nothing. He just stood and waited.

Daniel pointed and pulled the trigger only once, *bang*, and the bullet just sunk the same as it had done with Meredith. Smoke rose from the small hole in Faustus' cloak. Daniel's heart fell, smashing against the bottom of his stomach like a brick falling from a window. Ideas flushed through his mind as he weighed up every option. Finally, he had one. He had no choice, no other option. He put the gun to his own head. "You need me? Well, you can't have me if I am dead", he screamed at Faustus. Fear, anger, and confusion all muddled together in his voice. This seemed to work, and Faustus hesitated once again. It was nothing more than his eyes quickly looking past Daniel, but it was enough. It was all the encouragement that Daniel needed. He took a step forwards so that he was almost toe to toe with Faustus. "Back off!" Daniel shouted once again.

"I think not", Faustus said as he took a step forward. Now they were toe to toe. Faustus looked Daniel in the eye and said, "I don't think you will do it". Daniel heard a voice. *Only that was wrong.* He did not hear it; he felt it. Felt it as strongly as any voice he had ever heard. Not a voice that you can hear, not a voice from inside your head. This one came from the pit where his heart had dropped to, the very bottom of his stomach. This feeling spoke to him from there, a feminine feeling. An amused, giggling and laughing feeling. *Ohhh, this is great!* It felt with great amusement. *I dare you! I triple super quadruple mega dare you!* It felt like an overexcited schoolgirl buzzing around his stomach.

Faustus lunged at Daniel, and without thinking, he pulled the trigger.

*Bang.*

Pulling the trigger was the easy part.

Recovering was harder.

Daniel had tried to piece together what happened. He's still unsure. His head wound implied that the gun was pushed forward, the bullet grazing his forehead and luckily not seeming to have caused too much damage. He did not remember it that way though, he remembered the gun going off and then blackness, a void of nothingness.

He remembered dying in front of the door. Meredith and Faustus
laughing as he lay on the ground bleeding out.

Yet, a week later, he woke in the hospital.

# Now for the Reports

*Snippets from various sources.*

### **Burnham and Berrow Gazette.**

*Man found shell-shocked in town!*

Police and Ambulance services were called out last night to an old derelict house at the end of Marshfield Lane Bridgwater. Locals noted a disturbance at around 6.15pm and alerted the authorities, who arrived shortly afterwards. Upon entering the grounds, it was found that an unnamed man was suffering from shock and taken to the local hospital. After inquiries were made, it was established that the man had been investigating the house legally, and no further charges were made. ----------------------------------------------------------
------------------

Institute for Paranormal Affairs.
LOW PRIORITY.
Casefile: PHH87653

**Report:** The house "Egress" that sits at the end of Marshfield Lane has been unoccupied for several years now. We've had various reports of strange happenings over the years but have always put it down to the previous occupant.

Faustus Mcgovern and his follower(s) were previously occupying the house. Although we always found them to be harmless, the locals do not. Orgies, black masses and the usual nonsense have been reported. We have always forwarded this information to the police and explained that they are trying to recreate/perform a ritual that we don't believe exists. It is mostly just sexual practices and fiction bought to life. The current trustees have, though, asked that the house be thoroughly investigated due to constant disturbances. Reports have ranged from warm spots (strange) to cool spots. Doors being opened and slammed, power surges, and unexplained noises. These 'disturbances' are said to have started after the suicide of Mcgovern. It may be nothing. I have told them it will be investigated in due course, but it is a low priority. L/

---

Institute for Paranormal Affairs.
Casefile: Faustus Mcgovern.
DOB: 15/05/64
DOD: 17/07/12
**CLOSED CASE.**

Faustus Mcgovern has been on and off our radar for some time now. First appearing in the early eighties and continuing on and off for the rest of his life. He was looked into at various points during the eighties and nineties, and we declared him a fraud, but a case to keep an eye on. He has jumped from various cults and religions, almost exclusively the occult but is mainly harmless. Jumping from fiction to "non-fiction", he will follow Wheatley one moment and Crowley the next, bouncing from belief to belief. He seems to focus his energies on Lilith and writings about her. We believe he may be one of the few to have a complete collection of the Lilith Legend in his possession.

His followers seem to ebb and flow; they come and go. Some stay for a long time, others for a short while and then realise that he is a fraud. The one constant seems to be Meredith (surname unknown). Meredith met Faustus in the early two-thousands, around the time he fell from our radar. That may, or may not, be connected. Every time we tried to contact her, she had either been unavailable or her location unknown. We need to find out more about her - investigation needed.

Faustus's body was discovered alone and long dead in the basement of the house "Egress" on Marshfield Lane. Malnourished and cloaked in black, it was reported that he had been dead for at least two weeks. We had individual and independent checks done, and it was confirmed to be Faustus McGovern. Meredith was nowhere to be seen, and she has not been reported to us since.

L/

---

21/02/80

**Selling Potions:** These, upon being analysed, turned out to be nothing more than your average homoeopathy mixture. Snake oil from a snake, so to speak.

J/
31/10/85 | 21/06/87 | 21/12/89

**Sexual Gatherings**: Various orgies with followers throughout the years. The dates above are the ones that have been reported to us. The second two dates are the summer and winter solstices, the first, Halloween.

K/

13/02/93 - 17/06/97

**Seances**: Numerous! So many to mention individually. Not one of them actually worth a damn. Many junior members have been sent, and all have found the tricks used with ease. It is like he is not even trying any longer. Curiously, he has been doing them for free. So no criminal charges were ever made.

L/

??/??/00

**Rumour**: We have no idea where Faustus is, nor do we know with whom (if anyone). It was rumoured that he was in the USA and then Malta. I have been informed that he was hunting down the book "Legend of Lilith".

M/

15/07/05

**Update**: Faustus McGovern has returned and returned locally (rubbing our faces in it?) He actually made contact with us to claim that he is out of the # 'business'. I don't believe him, but we have no way to know for sure until something happens. I will inform the local police and pass on our notes (edited).
It is all we can do.

Some curiosities to note. He does have the Legend of Lilith! I have seen it, and he allowed me to read it. I could not read it all, of course, and much of it reads like the ramblings of a lunatic, but it seemed authentic. How were we never able to source a copy? Knowing it is genuine, how did we never find it? He has a massive collection of books, all on the occult. He told me it was just research and what he has collected over the years. I do not believe him - must keep a close eye on this.

I felt I was being watched the whole time I was there. I saw no other people, but I could not shake the feeling. I even asked, and Faustus, as polite as he could be, walked me around the house while telling his tale. Nothing, no sign of anyone.
Weird…

/L

---

Institute for Paranormal Affairs.
Casefile: PHH87653

This is my fault. I sent Daniel to investigate Egress, thinking it was nothing, and he ended up in the hospital. L tells me he was rambling about Faustus and Meredith (one dead, one unknown). He also claims to have shot himself but has only a scar on his forehead. No gun was located at the scene. The police believe it is shock - induced by what?? Why is black always black and white always white to them! - The medics said the same. They also said nobody else was to be found in or around the house. I checked out the house myself (with James), and it is run down and derelict, as you would expect from a place that has been sat empty for so long. I feel intensely guilty that I let Daniel go alone.

M/

Martin, don't be emotional in reports.
L/

I was emotional.

M/

# The Burning

## *2020*

Daniel sat at the desk in his house. It had been over five years, and now they ask him this? He had been found gibbering the in gardens, ranting about long-dead black magic preachers, skeletons in the basement and walking dead housekeepers. He had told everyone who would listen that he had killed himself, blown his brains all over the porch and watched himself die. He had felt the bullet that slammed into the side of his head. He had experienced his skull being opened like the tapping of a beer barrel. And, finally, as the world had turned to darkness. He had seen the mess his brains had left on the porch of the house.

It was true that he had a scar across his forehead and that his skull had been chipped. But brains across the porch? *Impossible.* Yet, he knew it to be true. He knew what had happened. If you spend enough time in a hospital with people telling you that what you know happened is actually impossible. You will eventually just decide to agree with them. It just makes life easier. *You do, after all, want to get out in the end.* So, you lie, and the lie becomes the truth. It is the lie that you tell everyone, and the memory of the truth would usually drift into darkness. Swallowed by the lie that became truth. Only this one never did; this truth still haunted him.

Lisa and her brother Martin had been the only ones who'd believed him. In his moments of doubt, he had wondered at their sincerity, but he knew better than that; he knew *them* better. They were, after all, his employers, but they were also his friends. He had taken the case file from them. The visits had started in unison and then trickled off so that only Lisa had come. She was his shining light in the worst of times, his guardian angel. She had sat there when he was rambling, she had sat through the ranting, and she had sat through the silence. Finally, when he had been considered well enough, Lisa had been the one to take him home. Pulling up in her ruby red mid-nineties Ford Escort Cosworth, she called it her pride and joy; he called her *glutton for punishment*.
She had dropped him at home, promising to visit the following day.

Days had passed, and finally, Daniel had found himself asking Lisa the question. A question that he had wanted to ask but had not really wanted to know the answer to. In the end, curiosity had got the better of him. *He had to know.* Daniel had almost blurted it out, throwing it out quickly to save himself from the embarrassment of choking. "What did you find in the house?" he had asked. Lisa had been dreading this question, she knew it would be coming, but she still flinched at it. She trusted Daniel. Lisa believed what he had told her. In his most vulnerable moments, she even loved him, loved what he had become, seeing a different side to him. A weakness that he had up until now kept well hidden.

Lisa had always known Daniel as a driven loner, doing everything his way. Daniel was machine-like in her eyes, brilliant at what he did but robotic and inflexible. Lisa believed in the supernatural, Martin believed in the paranormal. Daniel wanted to believe. He wanted to see the world through their eyes, but he was too stubborn, too realistic. He just could not take that leap of faith into the unknown. A practical solution was always involved. In Daniels defence, he had - *until now* - never failed to find one. Daniel had gazed into the abyss. What had looked back had not just stared into him; it had shaken everything that he had believed in.

Lisa and Martin had discussed how they would cross this bridge and deal with the problem she now faced. They had not reached any kind of consensus, both having differing views and opinions, neither knowing the answer. *If indeed there was an answer.* Her love for him made her want to lie, not to hurt but to protect. A white lie. How do you lie to the one you love? It was something that she would never understand. She had never done it, and she would not start now. Daniel was a man of reason, and he would have the facts dished out as they were. Complete, as they came, with no fancy extras. *Warts 'n all*, not sugar-coated. She just hoped he could handle them. "Nothing, we found nothing", she paused, waiting for a reaction. When Daniel just sat there, she continued. "The house was in better shape than you would have thought. It was still a mess, but not what you'd imagine after those years. They don't make them like that anymore, I suppose. But, other than that, nothing out of the ordinary". Daniel considered this for a moment. It was what he had expected, but hearing it aloud for the first time made him pause. "So what now?" he asked. To that question? Lisa had no answer for Daniel, perhaps, maybe even a Nightingale effect for both. Can *we ever know about these things for sure*? They were both adults, and when the flames of passion fizzled into embers, they knew it was over. Walking away from each other, still, as friends, knowing that things had burnt hot and fast, wondering what may have been, but never regretting what had been. Lisa had her reasons, and Daniel had not wanted things to end, but he understood. That had been thirteen months ago, the visits had stopped, and soon after, the phone calls had ceased. Daniel was alone with just his nightmares to keep him company.

Then this letter had arrived, their first correspondence in months, and it was about that *bloody* house Egress. Daniel read through the letter again; it did not make any sense. He reread it, and once more, just to be sure before he picked up the telephone and called the Institute. Old habits dying hard and muscle memory, he keyed in the number without a second thought and waited for it to be answered.

The Institute, the home of his employers and his ex-lover, just to make things a little more complicated. Having an experience that will scar you for life, hospital treatment and then screwing the boss. All in a day's work, right? *Well, if you are going to fuck up, you may as well do it cosmically badly.* The

Institute for paranormal affairs, established in 1942 and came to prominence in

1980. The Butchers Fountain had become notorious and famous when used as an example of proof of the supernatural. Many *experts* were called in, and they all called the place one of a kind. The only known proof of the supernatural anywhere in the world. Lisa and Martins father, Alex Fletcher, who had then been head of the Institute, decided to investigate.

Alex was an easy man to work for. Unlike his offspring, he did not consider anything supernatural to be real. He would have had far more in common with Daniel on that front. His attitude towards any case was that it was bollocks until he saw it with his own two eyes. He'd have chosen a less crude word in public; poppycock, hogwash or maybe humbug. They all added up to the same; he took a no-nonsense approach. Maybe it flows in generations. The grandfather of Lisa and Martin had believed, as they do, the father had not. But, like Daniel, Alex wanted to believe. Had he been born a few years later, he may have sported *Fox Mulder's* poster on a wall. *I want to believe; I really want to believe!* It had not taken him long to prove fraud in this case. A mixture of deception with a dash of trickery, and he had proven that the owners were behind it. *Case closed, job done*? Not quite.

The owners of the pub, a Mrs and Mr Batten, had sued. They had a whole host of people lined up who were willing to give evidence that they were not frauds and that the haunting was indeed real. The case rumbled on, the experts spoke, and many were discredited with Alex and the Institute's help. Many were not. Alex did not think the experts were terrible people, *not all of them anyway*. He just thought that people saw what they wanted to see or were not objective enough. Many of them genuinely believed the pub was haunted. Amazingly, the court had ruled in favour of the Battens. An English court had, for all intents and purposes, ruled that hauntings did exist.

There is an argument that no publicity is bad publicity. This was, in the case of the Institute, undoubtedly true. They were an organisation formed to investigate and deal with the supernatural. To many, they had proven the case against the Battens. Most who called them wanted them to prove things to be natural! They wanted the whistling pipes, creaky floorboards, and leaky windows. Alex had a problem. He did not like being called a liar, and he detested his report being disregarded in the manner that it had. So he made it his mission to prove them all wrong.

Locked away and paying scant attention to other things, he reduced the Institute's workforce to the bare minimum. It has been the same ever since. He had almost bankrupted them in the process, using every penny he had to prove a point. He bought a rundown pub of a similar age and size to what the Battens owned. And then he had set to work. He ripped the windows and doors out, replacing them with ones that were the same as those found at the Butchers Fountain. The inside was gutted, and very little, if anything, of the original pub remained. When the work was complete, the pub was a different building altogether. If you had seen the two side by side, you would not have thought it possible. The transformation was incredible. The ugly duckling had become the swan.

Alex had been unable to decide on a name, so he had given it two. One side of the pubs' signage read The Beautiful Duckling, the other, The Ugly Swan. He had then invited everyone involved with the case, *except for the Battens*, to come and stay for a weekend. He had been honest in his intentions with them all, telling them that he wanted to prove beyond all doubt that the Battens were frauds. Most of the invited guests came, the important ones did, and that was all that mattered. They had a night to remember on the first night, a night that scared every single one of them. They had seen and heard things that were only written about, things claimed to have proven the Batten case. Alex had to convince many of them to stay past the first night. Some had even wanted to leave in the middle of the night. The following day, he had shown them everything, every trick he had used, and every concealed device. The last evening, they slept - *if you'll excuse the phrase* - like the dead. Not a squeak was heard, not a crack creaked within earshot, and the windows did not wallow with the wind.

Alex then counter-sued the Battens. He sued them for damage to his name and business, even though that had been minimal. He sued them for costs. He sued them for the pub's cost, the refurbishment and anything else he could think of. If he could add it to the list, then he added it. Finally, his day in court came. The days dragged on, the case rumbled along. It is impossible to say in those early days what way the case would go. It could have been for or against. What swung it, dramatically, were the witnesses. People involved with the previous trial all gave statements. They all gave accounts that they did not now believe the Butchers Fountain to be haunted. They explained why, explained how they now understood the way things worked. That they had experienced all the tricks and secrets hidden behind cupboards or closed doors. The solicitor that had represented the Battens the first time around had even been a witness, claiming how now he felt he had been wrong.

Alex, and the Institute, had won the case. They had won everything. The Battens were broken. They lost their pub and savings. Jewellery was pawned, items and cars were sold. They were broke. Alex didn't give a damn. The Battens had thought they were clever, they had poked the Alex bear, and the bear had bitten back. Their name was mud, and then the press got hold of it. Histories were dug, stories were written, and skeletons unearthed from the darkest closets. Now they were broke, vilified and ridden with scandal. Alex didn't care, and he still didn't give a damn. The Battens left the country, fleeing to Europe. They had tried to run from their past, to leave it behind and start afresh. You can run from your past, and you can flee and never look back. You cannot run from your memories, as those will be with you forever. Mrs Batten died of a heart attack a year later. Mr Batten killed himself six months after that. Alex did not care; they had called him a liar. He should have cared, but he *still didn't give a damn.*

If luck were on Daniel's side, the phone would be answered by Martin, *if not...* Lisa answered the phone, and he paused and cursed under his breath. He took a second longer than he needed before speaking. "Hi Lisa, it's Daniel. I just got this letter". Lisa stopped him, butting in as he talked, impatience in her voice. "How could you not have told me?" she demanded of him. Daniel held the letter in his hand, and he clenched it into his fist. *How could you tell someone what you do not know?* He thought to himself. "I had no idea", he told Lisa.

"You had no idea?" Lisa scoffed, "No idea that you owned that bastard house?" It was the unsaid that had hurt the most. For the first time, Daniel had sensed that Lisa didn't believe him. They'd had their share of arguments in the past. They'd both said things that they had regretted. It was the tone in her voice. It was the way she had spoken to him. "Lisa, I would not lie to you. I had no idea! How the fuck could I have? I had the same information that you had". Daniel pulled the phone from his ear, angry at himself for cursing, angrier because he had sworn at Lisa. Daniel took a breath and tried once more. "Sorry, I didn't mean to swear", he said. It is not the swearing that bothered him; she had heard him swearing many times. It was the anger and the temper that had held its hand as he had sworn. He just did not want to admit that *Lisa* was the one who would not believe him. "Daniel, just phone the solicitors and get this sorted. I have had this case file for too long now. I just want it finished". That was how the call had ended. That was how he and Lisa had parted ways this time. They would meet again, but this left Daniel feeling cold, empty and alone.

Daniel hung up the phone and then called the solicitors, and sure enough, the house was now in his name. Left, apparently, *by a father.* A father that he had never met nor had ever known. "But", Daniel had said, shocked, "I've never known my father".

"Well, he had known you", came the unhelpful reply. A thought caught alight in Daniels mind. Like a piece of furniture from days gone by, it was soon aflame. "Don't tell me his name was

*Faustus*", Daniel asked, hoping beyond hope that the answer was no. Daniel heard the shuffling of pages over the phone. Files being checked and papers being read. "No, no. The name we have is Stephen Johnson", the voice replied. Unravelling quickly, everything Daniel had crossed uncrosses at speed, the relief lifting and leaving him feeling lighter.

A coiled spring of tension released itself as he worked it out in his head—

Stephen, not an anagram, not a known pseudonym, only a plain, boring

Stephen. "So, what do you want to do with the place?" the voice asked.

"Let it fucking rot", Daniel replied, ending the call almost at once. He

wanted nothing to do with it.

Then the nightmares started to recur. Nightmares and terrors of old finding their way back to the surface, and this time Lisa was nowhere to be found. When they had happened previously, she had been by his side in the hospital or, later, in bed. Now he woke alone in a sweat. He reached for the bedside lamp and checked every corner of the room for shadows that should not be, a darkness where there should have been light. A light where there should be only darkness. The nightmares were different now, they had the same core, but something was edging in from the side. As they peeled to reveal themselves for what they really were, the insides were different. It had always been the same, the visions and nightmares, just an old rerun of what he had experienced in the house. Now though, his mind was adding things, changing the experience. The tape that held his memories together had been spliced with another. He could not be sure. Was he *actually* remembering something that had happened? A memory so repressed it had stayed hidden for all this time, resurfacing only upon the discovery of new information? No, he pushed that to one side. The shadowy figure he had seen in his nightmares had been just that, a nightmare vision conjured from the darkest parts of his brain. Still, he'd had that feeling in his gut, the feeling like last time. He knew then what he had to do, knew what he wanted to do.

    The following morning Daniel watched as the clock ticked forward, a clock that is observed goes slower, but he did not mind. He had set his mind to something. The time it takes does not concern him; Daniel could always be *patient* if required. The clock tocked nine, and he grabbed his phone from the table. Reading the phone number from the letter, he dialled it and waited. He tapped his fingers across the table, it was a habit that Lisa hated, but he couldn't shake it. He was transferred and got the same talking voice as the last time, Mr Richardson. "Bulldoze the fucking thing" was what he had said, no reason given; that was his order, his command as it were. *Behold the voice of the great Daniel, and you will do as he commands.* "Knock the fucking thing to the ground and be done with it. Sell the land and donate the money to charity". The problem, something that he had not considered, would be the cost. "It's not going to be cheap," Richardson had replied. Daniel could ill afford to say donate the money to charity. He had wanted nothing to do with that house, and he could certainly not afford the kind of prices being spoken about now. *Flipety, Flapity, Flockety, FUCK*! "Fuck, so what can I do?" Daniel asked Richardson.

"Sell up, flog it, and forget it" had been his advice, but Daniel felt he couldn't do that. He did not want to take the risk of the house falling into the wrong hands. Daniel did not know why, but it felt like destiny. Like fate or wilp had intervened and placed the house in his hands. He wanted to be rid of the fucking place, but it had to be gone for good. Not sold on. It was not something he could pass on to someone else. His only choice now was what he should do with it.

Daniel found himself sat in his 2CV, once again. Five years on, the house and grounds remained unchanged. The nightmares he had been having were a perfect recreation of what he was now viewing. A mirage of the imaginary drawn over the reality. He could not help feeling that he was drawn to this place. Predestination on a journey he had no idea about, nor any way to escape, just along for the ride without any control, a passenger in his own life. Daniel shook the thought from his mind. *Wilp*. Fuck off, he did not believe in that either.

Daniel stepped from the car and into the moonlight. He headed for the boot and opened it, swinging up in the air, and he looked inside. Two full containers awaited him there. He had picked them up that afternoon. Taking them from the boot and placed them behind the car, he slammed the boot shut, not caring about the noise. There would be time for explanations later. He grabbed the containers and headed for the gate; it lay just before him and was unlocked. *Wilp* once again intervening? Or just coincidence. He had the key for the padlock, a collection from his past to be used when ready. He kicked the gate, and it swung open, squealing like a trapped mouse as it did so. The trees hung as he walked through them, the memories of years scattered in the leaves as they sagged with sadness. The stories they could tell, maybe this is one that they will remember, *perhaps it is not*. Time would tell, as it often does.

Calmness swam through Daniel as he walked the driveway. The weight of time and fear being lifted with each step he took. He should have been on edge, his nerves jumbling, but he just felt peaceful, tranquil. This was the place where his nightmares fermented; instead, he just felt nothing. Just a house and grounds left to the rotting of time. The house loomed large before him, begging him to enter. He could feel that the house held no danger. He had planned to work from outside, but as he drew closer, his confidence soared, and he decided that he would go inside.

Daniel approached the front door. Fear had wholly escaped him. Running away to join the trees, grounds, and gate, what will be will be. Yet, he knew deep down that he had to do this, that this is what had to be. As he kicked the front door, he expected resistance, a fightback from the house or a force within, yet nothing happened. The door creaked but gave in quickly enough. The wood had rotted with age, the lock broke with ease, the timber snapped in the frame, like a chicken's wishbone.

Daniel looked inside, seeing the hallway of his tormenter anew. It was the same as he had dreamt. Long dead and decaying from the inside. The first steps on his nightmare in this game called life. He shuddered and then stepped inside, expecting all of hell to break loose at once. Nothing happened. No ghosts and no visions. No knockbacks, not even a temperature change. Just a long-dead house sat alone on its grounds. The wind whistled through the hallway; it came from a room to the right. It was a howl he had heard many times in the past. It no longer spooked him, even here. Something long left open, a window frame that had maybe rotted to nothing, like Alex, Daniel does not care. He had no concern about the house. He made his way along the hallway and headed for the kitchen. The door at the far end on the left swung in a breeze, creaking and speaking wordless stories. Tales that are maybe not meant for human ears.

    The kitchen was as empty, just as he had expected it to be, as he had known it would be. No housekeeper waiting for him this time, haunting the kitchen and offering drinks. Only the smell of a long-dead past lingering on the walls and infecting his nostrils. The door to the basement was missing; a gaping hole remained. A doorway to his nightmares. Daniel thought about using the staircase and then decided against it; he did not want to push his luck. The house was dead, any life it once had was long gone, but the nightmares would always remain. He unscrewed the top of one of the cans and poured the petrol from within onto the steps.

    Daniel could hear the petrol dripping to the ground below, much of it being swallowed by the wooden stairs. He backed away from the opening, leaving a steady stream as he did so, covering the kitchen floor. Then he liberally covered the doorway and walls backing up into the hallway. One can empty; he just threw it aside and opened the second, continuing from where the first had emptied. Continuing to retrace his steps, making sure to cover everything in the fuel. If he couldn't knock the place down, he will burn the bastard to the ground. To hell with it. He stepped out onto the porch and finished emptying the can.

Daniel reached into his pocket and pulled his *Zippo* lighter from it. A relic of the past, from the days when he used to smoke. He sparked the Zippo, and after the third attempt, it lit. He looked into the hallway. "*Fuck you*", he said to the house before throwing the lighter. It was as the hallway burst aflame that he heard the voice in his head. "Shall we say a *spark*" replaying itself in his mind. The fire ripped through the walls of the house, a hot wave descended, slithering its way to the basement steps. The damage was done. He grabbed his phone, calling the fire brigade, but knowing it was already too late. The flames turned from yellow to orange, eventually settling on a crimson red. He felt it deep in his bowels. He has unleashed a hell; he had made such a terrible mistake.

# The Cloud

The fire brigade led to paperwork. The police also resulted in paperwork. Who knew that burning down a house you owned, a building standing on the grounds you owned, could be so damn complicated? Daniel should have known. Had he thought about it for more than thirty seconds, he would have known. Patient he could be; he also could be reckless. It was hardly the one-million-pound question on a game show. You can't go around burning down houses, even ones you own, without questions being asked.

A mountain of paperwork and questioning led to one single question that Daniel did not want to answer. *Why?* He could have answered. *Well, you see. The house is haunted, and I had a terrifying experience there, as you are undoubtedly aware. So after discovering it would cost too much to bulldoze it, I thought I would burn the fucker to the ground. That was the plan. I think it was a mistake.* He could not even claim it was an insurance job; heck, that would have been something. He had not insured the bastard, reckless and impulsive, not his best traits. Instead, he just clammed up and said nothing or next to nothing. He never wanted the grounds, neither did he want the house or its upkeep. It was the best that he could do. It was nothing good; it was hardly even adequate, but it was something, and they had let him return home in the end.

*Further enquiries pending.*

A white cloud had formed above the house; it went unnoticed by everyone. It was not a cloud formed by vapours of water; this was created from the mists of despair. Trapped for so long by the trickery, the skulduggery of the woman who it dared not name. Trapped for what had felt an eternity, but now it was released, now it could be free. Now it could play its own game. It would have some fun of its own, for it had been so long.

Grant placed the china doll outside his bedroom door and returned to bed. He lay his head back on the pillow and returned to counting sheep. He was twelve, nearly thirteen, and that doll still scared him. The dead glass eyes reflected the light back at him, or the cracked white skin revealing nothing underneath. Something about it gave him the heebie-jeebies. His parents had told him not to be so silly. He did not care about silliness, he only cared about what he felt, and the doll frightened him.

It had been so long, imprisoned for what was a timeless moment. Tortuous time in the void. Years could feel like minutes, but seconds could last decades. All fading into sand and then splitting to nothingness. Years may have passed in this world, but it was now ageless and impossible to guess for them. That may have been why it did not understand the feeling at first. It was a feeling long forgotten, lost in the ages of death and dust. It was a hunger, not for food, but for something else. It needed something more.

      Greg pulled it off and dropped the condom down the toilet, *plop*. He flushed and then cursed when the thing didn't disappear. *Bastard*. It was a cold night, and he felt the chill on his nipples. They hardened even more as he noticed. Now he would have to wait for the damn cistern to refill. The only thing that he hated more than condoms were children, so it was a sacrifice he was willing to make. He loved Grant, his son, of course. He just hated the idea of having another. Molly had floated the idea in her own unsubtle way; he was having none of it. He enjoyed the screwing but not the screaming. He'd once been young, dumb and full of cum. He was now older, a little balder and still full of cum. Molly would have added that he had all the stamina of a virgin teenager at a brothel. Greg didn't think of it that way. He'd had his fun, and that was all that mattered to him. Second flush, and the bastards were gone. *Ha, so long fuckers, enjoy purgatory*. He turned his back on the toilet, *forgetting to shut the lid*. Greg left the bathroom and looked at Grant's door. He saw the doll sitting outside. Shuddering, He returned to the master bedroom.

      Greg walked into the bedroom and looked at Molly. Molly lay on the bed just as she had been when he had left to use the toilet. Left breast exposed and smoking a cigarette. Her nipple poked from the areola, poking up, just saying hello. Unless? Unless she was still horny. They did look good enough to eat... No, Greg thought. He had jacked off that morning and screwed her tonight. That was enough for him, and besides, the doll had stolen the mood. He never once gave a thought to what Molly may have wanted. She flicked the ash into the ashtray without looking. Some of it missed and scattered on the bedside table. "He's put that damn Doll outside the door again", Greg said as he crawled back up into bed. "The thing gives me the willies". Greg laughed at this, his humour... Maybe he had gotten older and dumber. He lay back and scratched his balls. Molly stubbed out the cigarette and shuffled over; she placed her head on his chest. "Your mother bought it for him, and you know I can't stand it either", Molly replied.

"Can't we just get rid of it?" Greg asked her, although he knew the answer already. They had been over it a few times before. "If we give in to him on this, then where does it stop?" Molly answered. "Next thing, we are checking under his bed for monsters. He is almost thirteen, for goodness sake".

The cloud hovered and waited. It knew that its moment would come. It was learning, learning everything anew. What had once been second nature to it had now become a learning experience. It had to be wary, it was still young and could not hazard anything going wrong, but it also had the confidence to strike. An arrogance built up from felt like years of waiting. It watched the car thief with eager interest. Could a thief be of use to it? Maybe it thought. Could it even use the thief? Yes. It made its way, floating upon nothing, so it was behind the man. The man paid no attention. He was fixed upon the crime he was committing. The cloud pounced and was absorbed into the man. Like water on a sponge, it seemed to just pull the cloud inwards, in through his thick black jacket and into his body. Further still, it delved, tunnelling onwards and deeper. Tunnelling past the flesh and bones of the human. It was looking for something hidden deep within. His essence, his soul. And, it had found it, and now it would consume it.

The man stood gormless, dumbstruck and in a trance. He suddenly lurched forward, smashing his head upon the car. The thief lifted his head and stood as the blood dripped down his forehead. A stream that was tasteless to him made its way to his mouth. He slammed his head repeatedly into the car, one final hit, and the skull cracked open. The thief's body fell to the floor, blood seeped from the head, depositing itself down a nearby drain, just like a toy that has broken and then thrown to one side. The cloud left the body lying on the floor; it had served its purpose.

It now watched the house windows as the lights went out, plunging the house into darkness. Its time had come. Entering the house would not be a problem. In times gone by, it would have used caution and tools of the trade. Now it could just drift under the doorway, the smallest of gaps providing an opening. Nowhere could be safe from it. Besides, had it needed, it now knew a thief. Had the door not been possible, it would have found another entrance; it always would. It always could.

The house inside was clean and tidy without being fastidiously neat, everything had a place, and everything was in it. The cloud looked around, looking for something it could use. Reckless it was not, and careless was something it would never be. It had not been rash when it was one; now, it was three. The souls of three combined as one. There was nothing it could see in the porch or front room, so it floated towards the kitchen. It did not know what it was looking for. A thought that swept through what could be called its mind and urged it to learn a new skill.

The handle of a knife sat in a block holds its interest for a moment; can it lift it? It is not so sure. It could control the thief, but a human is a different thing. It feels the bluntness of self-doubt swopping inside. The human felt natural. It was, after all, what it had once been. This was metal and wooden. The wood had once held life but no longer. It looked at the handle, taking its time, concentrating all its energy upon it. The cloud coiled outwards with tiny fingerlike gasps of mist. The knife wobbled in the block as the wafts tried to grasp it. It can do this, for it is legion; for it is many.

The knife suddenly shot from the block, flying across the room. The whiskers from the cloud followed it at speed, much like the smoke in a wind tunnel. It had to concentrate everything it had on controlling it so that it stopped before it could clatter and fall to the ground. It willed the knife back to the kitchen side. It floated on the misty cloud across the kitchen and back to the work surface. The knife would not do. It needed something more familiar, something it had more in common with, something it could relate to. Something that it could understand from its past. The cloud drifted from the kitchen, making its way up the stairs towards the bedrooms.

As with the downstairs, the upstairs landing was clear of clutter and mess. The only thing in the hallway was a single doll propped against the wall. It took a moment for it to recognise what it was looking at. Its first thought was that a small child was looming on the landing. Had it been able to speak, it would have exhaled an excited *oh* as it realised what it was seeing. This was perfect; it thought to itself as it hovered the hallway. Better than perfect, it is excellent. This must me *wilp* in action. It let itself be pulled into the doll; it is as if the child's toy took a drag on a virtual cigarette. The white smoke being inhaled through every crack on its body. Every crevice and aged indentation an opening it could use. The doll twitched, and the head fell forwards, resting against its stuffed chest. Slowly at first, it found its feet, wobbling but steadying itself with an arm against the wall. This action came naturally to it. It was just a human analogue, smaller but essentially the same as the thief. The arms and legs moved freely, the stuffing long past its use-by date easing any resistance there may have once been. The head lifted and bobbled from side to side as the doll moved and made its way along the hall.

The master bedroom door creaked open as the doll pushed it, a quiet squeak but a noise nonetheless. The doll made its way into the bedroom, a lightness of foot as it stepped on the plush carpet. It could feel every touch, it had not realised it before, but outside of this doll, it had lost all sense of feeling. Inside the doll, it could feel everything. Was the doll in itself special? It did not think so. It was just something it could inhabit, a thing that it could relate to? It thought about the knife, was that why it could not handle it? It lacked feeling as it had lifted it, unable to judge how hard to pull to release it from its block? Everyone used little things in life and could not realise how important they were until you had them no more. It seemed likely, it would have to experiment in the future. For now, it had other plans.

Greg and Molly now lay asleep in the room, oblivious of the doll that crept toward them. Molly dreamt of a life without Greg. They had married shortly after leaving school. Schoolyard romance blossoming into young adult love. And that, in time, evolved into unexciting normality. She loved Greg, sometimes. Most of the time... Greg's dreamt of a life where he could do what he wanted, when *he* wanted, carrying Molly as an accessory of sorts. Something to be there when he needed it, but not when he wanted to have fun. Grant barely registered with either of them.

The doll had by now snuck to the side of the bed and arched its head backwards. Two wisps of cloud escaped its enamel mouth, drifting upward to the ceiling and then back down, a single puff for each human soul, the rest saved for the doll. It wanted to watch; it enjoyed watching. The ultimate entertainment *coming soon from CSC Entertainment is yours for the new super low price of only one human soul.* The bodies contorted for a moment, moobs, boobs, and bellies rising in the air held aloft only by their neck and feet. Then they flopped downwards back onto the bed, their breathing had stopped, and they are motionless.

Molly sat up suddenly, a flash of action, and she was upright. In one motion, no arms were needed. She just lifted her upper body with ease. She rolled over and straddled Greg. Greg lay unmoving, still, and dead. Molly tried to stimulate him, trying to wake him from his eternal death. She ran her hand down the front of her body, sliding it down between her legs. Writhing and squirming as she did so, Greg sprung to life, one instant dead and the next, the undead. He grabbed her by the hips, and they twisted together as he grew into her. The headboard crashed against the wall, hitting it so hard that the ashtray fell from the bedside table, smashing in pieces on the floor below. Ash flailing in the room. Butt flopping up in the air on the bed and butts down to the ground below it.

Grant woke. He was startled at the noise. He was shaken from his dreams, unsure of what is real or still a waking dream. The darkness lifted from his vision and mind as the next bang hit. *Bang*! Once again, a continuous rapping of noise. The banging, the squeaking of the bed, and the groaning mixing eventually forming into the festival known as fucking. Like many his age, Graham has heard his parents making love. He is not sure what this is, but it is, unlike any lovemaking he has heard! Crashing, banging, squeaking and moaning once more fills the vacant airwaves.

Grant moved towards his bedroom door. He took it slow, not really wanting to know what lay beyond. They were screwing, so what? He'd - *unfortunately*- heard it before. Why did he feel the need to look, the need to peek at what should not be seen? The feeling deep in his belly that something was wrong. The need to just take a peek into the dark and look. He opened the door gingerly and looked into the hallway, flicking on the light as he did so. It never occurred to him to look down, to look at where the doll had once been placed. Had he done so, he may have lived to tell his tale, the story of his parent's death. Greg and Molly's last great fuckathon. As he walked the hallway, he felt every bang on the floor and walls. Vibrations flowed from his feet, up through his body and eclipsing in his head. Every squeak screamed stop, yet every groan and moan seemed to egg him forwards, pushing him toward the door of the master bedroom. *Hey Granty Wanty, wanna go peek? See ya first set of boobs that you can remember?* He stood before the door with a hand outstretched; he placed a hand upon the door and pushed.

Grant stepped into his parent's bedroom. He repeatedly blinked as he tried to get his eyes to adjust to the darkened room. The room seemed unnaturally dark, like a darkness has crept from the cracks in the plastering. The light from the hallway should have been shining through. He blinked some more, knowing deep down that it would make no difference, yet still, he tried. One of the bedside lights switched on, and it felt like he was blinded for just a second. Molly had leant over and flicked the switch. She still straddled Greg, but the first thing Grant noticed is the colour. Red, a blood-red that would be burned into his mind. Molly leant forward toward Greg and bit him on the chest. She lifted back up, pulling and ripping at his skin, yanking it upwards with her teeth. It sounded like Velcro ripping. She chewed on the skin, eating some and spitting more. The sheets soaked up yet more of the blood as it flowed freely from the two of them.

Grant stood flabbergasted, unable to move, not knowing what to do. His feet felt like they were stuck in the mud at the local beach. Greg looked over, eyes dead and white, just like the dolls, but without the reflection. He smiled at his son, licking his lips as he did so. Grant could see the blood-red lips, discoloured by the blood of life. Grant just stared, stupefied by it all, his immature brain unable to take it all in. Deadlocked and inanimate like a human statue. Molly flopped back, her head by Greg's feet. She lies there. Grant can see where chunks had been ripped from her breasts, chewed or eaten; he does not care. She patted the bed as if inviting him to come and join them. There was no emotion in her face, her eyes white and dead like his fathers. Grant finally released, something gave both up top and down below. He pissed himself and, at the exact same moment, started to scream. A curdling scream rising from the pit of his stomach as he is freed from the imaginary mud that had held him. Grant turned to run, and that was when he saw the doll standing, watching him. Looking straight at him, head at an angle that would have been impossible before.

The doll looked at him, and then the mouth cracked open. Shiny porcelain shards imitating teeth, an opening where there should have been just painted lips. A selection of gravestones inside its mouth. All small, white and ceramic. Its left arm reached up and pointed at Grant, smiling its toothy grin, pointing, and staring with its dead eyes. Instinct took over, and Grant ran for the door. He could not stay here in this blood-soaked sexual bedroom from hell. He made it through the doorway, but then he felt pain deep in his ankle at the very moment he thought he was free. He collapsed to the floor and looked down toward his foot. The doll had bitten into his ankle, and it was now shimmying up his leg. Like a spider up a drainpipe, only there was no water to flush this one out. The blood flowed freely from his ankle to the floor. He struggled to free himself, but the toy doll was too strong, too unnatural with its grip. He kicked at it with his good foot but missed it completely. It crawled the length of Grant, all the time holding on as he tried pushing away using his uninjured leg, trying to escape. Digging his foot into the ground to push himself backwards. The doll was relentless. It just crawled and worked its way up, the fingers of the thing like little spikes digging into Grant's bony young leg. It reached Grant's neck and bounded for it. Its teeth quickly ripped into it. Fingers like needles piercing the skin around it as the doll held tight. Thankfully for Grant, the rip severed the carotid artery, and death came quickly. His body lay limp on the floor as the banging restarted.

# The Psychic

Daniel slept, and unlike the sleep that had plagued him for half a decade, this had been a night of good sleep. This was sleep where he did not wake sweating. Not waking to feel his heart beating in his neck, trying to escape his body. He did not feel the need to check for something slithering in the corners of the room. Did he dream? He supposed he must have; he did not - *for the first time in an age* - remember. He sat up and flopped his legs over the side of the bed, slipping his slippers on as he did so. He really could not remember the last time he'd had a dreamless night. Grabbing his dressing gown from the floor, It had fallen from the bed; he wrapped it around himself and shut out the cool morning air. He made his way downstairs and to the kitchen.

His daily caffeine intake was needed and needed quickly. Daniel turned the radio on and switched to the local station, listening for the news. He waited to hear if anything interesting had happened, wondering if his torching of the house would make it; *it didn't*. The usual gossip and nonsense, nothing more than regurgitated crap to feed the few who listen. It was the same most mornings. He would turn on the radio in the mornings to add some noise to the day. After listening for 10 minutes, hearing more adverts than anything else, he would turn it off. Tomorrow would be the same, as was yesterday. Like many relationships, a vicious circle of love and hate. Though not the one he and Lisa had shared. That thought reminded him of his plan for the day, he had to call the Institute, but he did not want to speak to Lisa again. *Welcome to the breakfast show, Will Daniels plan work? Will he get his wish? How will he make sure he gets what he wants? Tune in after these sponsored messages...*

Daniel headed to the hallway and then to the shelf that held the telephone and a few books. *The shelf by the front door that held the landline telephone, soon to be extinct and only available for viewing in your local museum.* Daniel looked through the pile of books, looking for one particular book. He found it, opening it, and flicked the pages stopping halfway through. Daniel ran his finger down the list of names in his contact book and stopped upon reaching Martin's name, "Bingo", he said to himself as he thought about where he would put the books once the phone was gone. Keeping the book open at the page, he walked back to the kitchen and sat at the table. He got his mobile and keyed in the number. The phone rang, and he put it on speaker, placing the phone on the table. Martin answered the phone, much to Daniels delight. He had feared Lisa would answer. Lisa and Martin worked in the same office, at the same desk. It would not have been unlikely for her to have seen Daniels name flash upon Martins phone. Maybe she had, he thought.

"Martin, Daniel", he said, "I am calling about the house. I've sorted it".

"Sorted it?" Martin replied, "Bloody hell, mate, that was quick. What did you do, find a buyer?"

"I burnt the fucking place to the ground. It's done, gone. fuck it!"

"You did what!" Martin laughed, "It's a bit unconventional, but I suppose if it works. It did work, didn't it?"

"I didn't have a nightmare last night, so it's a start", Daniel replied.

"No nightmares? That's wonderful", Lisa added. Daniel realised he is on speakerphone too. "Hi, Lisa, uh yeah. No nightmare, singular. It is a start", Daniel said, wanting the call to end quickly now as this was not how he had planned it. "So what happened?" Martin asked, "anything unusual?"

"Other than you becoming an arsonist", Lisa added.

"It was unusual to spend the evening between the fire service and police station, but no, other than that, nothing strange", Daniel said. Adding, "It was strange, almost like the house was willing me to do it. I did not intend to go inside at first, just to burn it from outside. When I got there, I just felt a pull and ended up starting with the kitchen and covering the hallway in petrol".

"You really did go for it!" Martin said as he laughed, "How did the police feel about it?"

"Unimpressed would be the word I'd use. The fire service felt the same", Daniel answered sheepishly.

"I'm not surprised", Lisa said, "And you should not be surprised either if they lumber you with the bill!" Daniel groaned inwardly, another cost he could ill afford. He hoped it would not come to that. "I don't want to be a downer here", Martin added; the laughter had departed from his voice. "But, do you really think it was a good idea to burn what we didn't understand?" It was a good question, one that Daniel would usually have considered. "Fuck it, it's done. I couldn't give a shite about the rest; let 'em bill me. I am just glad it is out of my life", Daniel said, meaning it. Daniel ended the call by saying goodbye and promising to keep in touch both professionally and informally. Martin's question had concerned him. He would have usually agreed, and it went against his nature to want to destroy what he didn't understand. Daniel thought about it for a second or two, then decided that he was right, *fuck it*. He clicked the kettle and put the radio back on. Another coffee was in order.

The radio played, and with his coffee made Daniel sat back down. Mindless, beat less drivel plays first, ending in a monotonous noise that seems to defy song writing basics. Not that he knew about song writing. *Taste*, he thought, he'd never had any, and he still didn't understand the trends. Adverts came next, come to our car wash, buy your beds here. The usual shite, nothing of any interest, just alleged bargain after bargain, then the news begins. The news report was what Daniel was waiting for. He always listened to the news. It was an addiction, a bad one. He'd listen to the news in the morning, and it was a sure-fire way to start the day in a shite mood. Politicians who were unable to keep their pants (or knickers) on. Death, robberies, muggings and all that jazz. It was the best way to start a day feeling that humanity was a little bit wayward, a touch broken. A bad habit, an addiction that he could not quit.

The cloud hovered, *dormant*. It had been fed and was satisfied, full after gorging on new souls. When it had killed the souls before - *for it did not think of them as human* - they had merged with it, become one with it. It felt that it had more strength, more control. Was that because of them or simply because it was fed? It could not be sure. There was said to be much power in innocents; maybe the youngest of them held the key, maybe innocents were vital. *No*, something told it that was wrong. It was not the innocence that mattered. It was the corrupting of them, degrading them until they were no more. Ripping their souls apart and gouging upon them until they were no longer welcome in either Heaven or Hell, they were the unwanted, the unwelcome. They were now all outcasts. Unwelcome in the many planes of existence.

Martin and Lisa sat at the desk that they shared. Martin on one side and Lisa on the other. Lisa was dressed in a dress suit, a neckerchief in black that her hair fell around. Martin in a plain and boring navy suit and tie. Why did they get dressed up when it was just them in the office? Professionalism, wanting to look good? It mainly was habit. There was a split almost right down the middle that separated the two sides, Lisa's side being chaotic, and Martin's all ordered and neat. Lisa didn't need systems for everything. She could find order in chaos;
Martin needed order. Though both were good at what they did and either
chaotic or ordered, they would very much work in sync without much effort. "I'm concerned about this", Martin said. He looked across the desk at his sister.

"About the house?" she asked; it had been bothering her too. She looked up from her paperwork, "I agree, burning it down was not a good idea". Martin leant forward, his elbows resting on the desk. Fingers of his hands crossed together, he rested his chin on them. "The house is haunted. We know that. So why didn't it, or its *occupants*, put up a fight? Why did it let Daniel burn it to the ground?" He asked. Knowing it was not a question that either of them could answer with any certainty. "Do you think it could have stopped him?" Lisa said. "He would have been pretty determined to go through with it. You know what he can be like".

"It does not feel right. It feels too easy", Martin said. "We know the house was haunted, and we know that it was not linked to any event like a lunar cycle or any pattern we could see, right?"

"Right, nothing we could see", Lisa replied, stressing the final four words.

"So then why did it die? Did it move on? Can it do any of those things?
If it can't, and I certainly don't think it could, why did it not fight back?"

"It has been troubling me too", Lisa said, "You should know that". Martin knew, if it had been bothering him, then he knew it would have been bothering her. In many ways, they were different. Sometimes, though, they could be spookily similar.

David stood alone outside the police station, a large file in one hand and a cigarette in the other. His blue jeans and shirt keeping him warm in the cool mid-morning breeze. He took a long drag of the cigarette and blew the smoke into the air, watching it as it drifted. He's older now, and if smoking kills him, then so be it.

He'd led a decent life, maybe even a good one, so what did it matter now? He had nobody dependent on him, nobody to care for. If he lived or died, it would be his choice. He would rather bow out on his terms than have something like cancer or dementia. He opened the file and flipped through the pages, shaking his head and then he closed the file. What really is the point, he thought to himself as he threw the cigarette to the floor. He had worked as a policeman all his life, working his way through the ranks. Closer to retirement now than when he had first joined the force. The world just did not seem worth it at the moment.

  He shook his head once more. Trying to shake the thoughts that clouded his mind. He had never seen anything like this. Boy killed with a china doll, parents screwed and ate each other while fucking, literally fucked and ate each other to death. "Jesus Christ", he said to nobody but himself, "Jesus fucking Christ". Then there was the car thief found just down the road. Found with his face smashed to pieces, was it connected? Was he just caught by the owner of the car? Could it have been some kind of fit? David lit another cigarette and took another long hard drag.

  Crystal, *not her real name*, sat and dealt the tarot cards. The cards were not needed. They were, like her name, a prop, a part of an act. They had mocked her when she was known as Grace, Grace with the crystals telling the future. So she had changed her name to Crystal, Crystal with the crystals. If you can't beat them, join them. Besides now, when they took the piss, it was good for business. The crystals didn't matter. The tarot meant nothing. Glass balls were okay as doorstops and Palmistry. Well, there were better things to do with your hands. She pulled her hair up, tied it in a loose ponytail, and dealt the next card, placing it carefully upon the table.

Crystal was not a fraud; she did have a gift. She could not tell the future, that was *wilp*, but she could read people and speak to spirits. She had been able to do both and discovered a talent for it at the time of puberty. The talent for the theatrical had developed shortly afterwards. Some of it was because of necessity, most of it because she enjoyed it. Like many gifted people, it was both a blessing and a curse. The sadness of it all was the scourge. People would visit, and she would hear the most distressing stories from both the living and the dead. She had never charged anyone. The services she gave were free, given willingly and voluntarily. It was how she had been able to lay low and never get involved with any groups that wanted to test and control the people like her. She had kept it honest, and because of that, she had drawn no outside interest.

Crystal turned the final tarot and saw death staring back at her; she would have to seek them out. The girl had come to her in the early hours, screaming and begging to be saved. There was nothing that she could do for her, save help her move on when it was the right time. But she may be able to help others, and, after all, isn't that what having a gift is all about?

# The Reports - Cont.

## **Somerset Tattler.**

*Murder? Blazes and Mayhem in local town!*

*Last night a known car thief was found dead in Marshfield lane. Brutally beaten and left dead on the pavement, the police have no leads. Our star reporter Janice Windlow was on the scene quickly, ready to bring you the latest updates.*

Arriving on the scene, the house at the end of the once quiet Marshfield lane had stopped smouldering. The fire service had said that no further action was being taken. As I arrived, the mayhem had already finished. It is hard to believe that this small sleepy seaside town, especially this tired little lane, could have been scenes of such violence. Previously the house was set ablaze by Daniel Johnson of the Institute for Paranormal Studies. I have contacted them for comment, but they had not returned my calls or emails at the time of going live. What started with fire has seemingly exploded into a night of madness and chaos. With at least four deaths!

The only name we have at the moment is that of Thomas Hopkins. He was a known thief in the area, and few will shed any tears at his

demise. His body was found on the pavement next to parked cars. The head had been smashed to a pulpy mess! Was it a revenge attack? Did someone catch him breaking into
their car? We can only speculate at the moment, but judging from what I have seen in this reporter's eyes, it was a brutal murder. Sources informed me that they are not yet treating it as murder. How that can be, this reporter will never know!

My source also tells me that what they found in the house at 37 Marshfield Lane was unlike anything they had seen before. They described to me a scene too horrific to detail in this report. A couple who had seemingly been having sex and bitten and eaten each other to death. Then their young son being killed. I had the details described to me, and I found them hard to cope with, even with my strong stomach!

Be well readers, and stay safe out there! I'll be here to bring you the latest news only on BandBTat.co.uk. ----------------------------------------
----------------------------------------

INTERNAL.
TO: David.watson@BPD-internal FROM: Dr.Richards@BHD-internal
Subject: Marshfield Lane.

Hi David, Doc Richards here.

Preliminary reports from Marshfield are a strange one (I seem to be saying that a lot these days. I shall tell you about it over a pint when we next meet). I'll keep this in layman's terms, as usual. You can collect the official report tomorrow.

Thomas Hopkins. This one initially looks like he was pushed or hurled forwards into the car. I am sure you don't need me to tell you that! Even a layman could have put it together. It is pretty fascinating in some ways. The officer on the scene told me there were no signs of a second party. My initial medical work confirms this. It is possible that the initial blow was what killed Hopkins and that he was caught by surprise. Possible, but unlikely. Have you ever tried to grab someone by the head and push them forwards over a distance of two/three feet? You need some strength as they naturally tense up. I thought about drugs, but his bloodwork was clean. I can see no signs of a struggle. I can only conclude at this moment that there is a possibility of some kind of seizure. Though, I'll admit it would be like nothing I have seen nor read about.

37 Marshfield.

This one is horrible. Once again no signs of an outside party. Greg and Molly Chapman did indeed have sex and killed each other. What is strange (there is that word again) is that the injuries appear to be post mortem. That can't be right, but I can only follow the evidence. It's not as if someone would imitate sex while killing them. I don't see how it would even be possible!

The son (Grant) is tragic, he was killed shortly afterwards, and yes, the doll was used as a weapon. Odd though it undoubtedly is, whoever did this tried to make it look as if the doll had crawled up his leg. The only saving grace, if you can call it that, was that he died quickly. The poor lad must have been terrified before death. It is never pleasant in any circumstances, but when it is a child!

Note. You should look at that reporter from the Tattler! How can she know so much! Have you read this morning's online report! Who is her source? She knows too much about this!

---

TO: Mark.Wtkns@BDP-internal
FROM: Steve.Tennings@BFD-internal
Subject: Marshfield Lane Fire.

Mark.

I've been chucking this one about for a while. Honestly, mate, I don't have the time, resources or energy to pursue this. I know by the book we should do, but I can't spare any more resources to prosecute someone for burning his own property.

Yes, it was a pain in the ass, and yes, I got called out, so I should be more annoyed. Did you see him? He seemed like he had made the worse mistake of his life! I don't think we will be having any more problems with him. I'd recommend a stern warning, threats of legal action etc… and leave it be.

Cheers

Steve.

# The Church

The round Church sat alone on, basking in the autumn sun. *Our Lady and the English Martyrs* already filling up for the daily service. Catholic services for the flock are held daily for those that want them. Some go because they believe, others because they feel they have to, many go because they need to.

John hated Churches, and if he had believed in any of the spiritual mumbo-jumbo, he would have thought himself a creature of Hell. Heaven, he figured, must be a place of preaching and boredom. Not that he was evil. He'd just rather have sex, rock and roll and alcohol. He could live without the drugs. Churches repelled him, and he could feel his spirit dragging itself away, wanting to stay free of it all. This was all psychological. He was not demonic. John was not a creature of the underworld. He just did not like going to Church. Holy water did not boil when he went through the doorways. Crosses did not fall upside down. Had they served alcohol or let him watch the match, then he would have had a different view. But, as they did not, he stuck to disliking them.

John always went to Church because Mary went to Church, and for all the repulsions he felt for the place, *and they were legion,* he would walk Heaven or Hell for his Mary. They had met at school and been together ever since, never once regretting the decision they had made. It was the *truest* of true love.

Like anybody, they'd had ups and downs, but they were happy, eternally happy.

Except for John, when it came to going to Church.

John rolled his eyes as they walked into the Church. *Oh God, why does it have to be a busy one*, he thought. There were usually ten, fifteen people maximum here on a Sunday, today there was at least thirty. He groaned inwardly. He suppressed the noise as best he could. Mary stood beside him. He looked over; he could see a glow in her eyes. She loved the busy ones, and he loved that glow, it was a shine that radiated from her, and it would usually always make him feel better about himself, just *not* on a Church day. They had no children. God worked in mysterious ways, *apparently*, had meant that he was infertile. Still, they were both happy, and that was what really mattered. They made their way to a pew and sat down, waiting for the service to begin. He looked down at her feet! If only the bible thumpers knew. She was wearing her Church heels. If nothing else, at least he had that. He loved it when she heels up. Dressing up and not down for Church, they all had no idea that she was naked under that dress, save for the stockings.

*Stockings and Heels, it makes Church worth it, almost.*

John leant back, looking up toward the ceiling. It was a ceiling, nothing fancy, nothing special, just circular and dreary. It was a ceiling he had looked at more times than he cared to remember. Churches worldwide are built, sometimes with the most spectacular murals, and he got a boring one to visit weekly. Still, he had the heels. The woodworking was excellent. He looked at the joins and the large wooden beams that were built to last. He may not have faith in God and the Church, but whoever had built this knew how to make it last. He could appreciate good workmanship. It was then that he noticed the haze, a slight blur of what looked like a mist. He thought it is his eyes at first, playing tricks, but it thickened and shimmered slightly. He was reminded of the old days when you could smoke in a cinema, drifting whiteness in the centre of the ceiling. Thinking it was smoke at first, he was about to raise the alarm, but then he looked at it; it was hypnotic. The way it seemed to move but didn't move. A heat haze seemed to be covering it. It made it flicker and appear to be alive. There was something about its swirling. He looked back down; The service was starting, *urgh*. Preaching and lecturing, sod it; if it was smoke, at least it would liven things up. He kept looking up as the service continued, watching as the cloud thickened.

Crystal departed from the bus and waited outside the Institute. She always used public transport to go everywhere, enjoying the rides if nothing else. She would watch as passengers arrived and departed. They would wonder what their lives were going to bring. In most cases, she could have made a welleducated guess, or at the very least, she could have got an inkling of what things would be like. You make your own luck, positive outlook, positive life, was what she had always believed. There was some truth in it, she supposed, maybe a little. She was optimistic in her own life, forever trying to see the good in things even if everything else seemed to be spiralling downhill. She smiled a bittersweet smile as she stood looking at the plaque of the Institute. She had avoided people like this for her whole life, people who would judge, test, and be cynical of her. Always asking questions and looking for a trick where there was none. She looked for longer than needed as she forced herself to do what she had for so long avoided. She pushed the door open, took a long deep breath and stepped inside.

David sat at his desk and took a sip from the coffee cup; it was lukewarm now but still drinkable. The timeline is wrong. He knew it is wrong; he just could not piece it together correctly in his head. Just looking at the facts as he lays them out on the table. Mother and Father killed each other, *but the son*, the son, was wrong. He leant back in his chair and closed his eyes, trying to block out all the noise, locking himself in his own thoughts.

*Let's start with the facts.*

Distasteful as it may have been, *pardon the pun*. Fact number one is that the parents fucked and fed on each other until they had died. Finishing off with ripping off each other's throats, *similar* to the son, but not the same.

The second fact, the boy was killed using the china doll. The doll must have been modified. Somehow, the mouth opened, and... And, this was where David started to get lost. Richards had said the doll was the weapon used. Bites on the ankle, ripping, marks on the legs, and bites on the neck. Fact number three, the doll had been found downstairs by the kitchen door. Facts number two, three and one cannot add up; they do not go together. It does not compute. The boy had been killed upstairs, the dolls head did not move, it can't bite, and the parents had never left the bedroom. And yet, the doll had all the proof of being the weapon used. There was not enough blood in the rest of the house unless the weapon had been taken. But then, why leave the doll? Something was missing, a part of the equation that was unknown to him. There were no signs of anyone else being in the home; there were no signs of a break-in. Something, a final part of the puzzle, eluded him.

John watched as the cloud thickened. He seemed to be the only person who had spotted it. The rest of the Church continued with the service. Amen, praise the Lord, Kumba - *fucking* - ya. He knew it was not smoke; he or somebody else would have smelt it by now if it were. No, this was a cloud forming inside the Church. That can't be right. He looked over the beams and could see no moisture, a dry cloud of nothing. The type you may find in a disco or nightclub. It was definitely growing, getting larger and less translucent. He continued to watch, glancing and watching with fascination.

Lisa did not have time for this; she grumbled to herself. Cranks, crackpots and con artists, why did they always gravitate to her? Was it her gender? Quite probably, they thought it would be easier to pull the wool over her eyes, maybe? Well, they were wrong. If they wanted an easy mark, then they would get neither here. If they had liked to at least be heard by someone sympathetic, then by basing a choice on gender? *Ha, wrong move, sucker*. Martin was who they should have picked, but they always gravitated to her.

*Psychics! Don't make me laugh.*

There had been something in this one, just something that she had said.

Lisa had loaded up the file on her PC, checking what they knew about this Crystal. Crystal, nee Grace, Pickforn, aged thirty-six, had been on the system for most of her adult life. Was Crystal gifted? Maybe, maybe not. She was known to the Institute, but she was of little interest, she did not make money, and there had been no complaints against her. Crystal kept herself to herself, bothering nobody. As far as Lisa could see, Crystal had no criminal or civil complaints. There was certainly nothing in the public domain. They would have kept out of each other's way. Crystal not doing anything to draw attention, and because she did that. There was no real need for the Institute to have made any contact. Live and let live; they could not investigate everything. Here she now was, contacting them about something that she should not have known about. So why had she approached them now?

"I know all about the man and the house", Crystal had said in the telephone call. "I think you care, or cared, for him. I want you to know he is in danger". It was always possible that Crystal has read the newspapers and added things together, coming to this conclusion. A little guesswork here and there, she would not have been the first. Lisa and Daniel's past was not hidden, something tucked away in the pages of a book and for them to be ashamed of. The house getting burnt down was in the local press. Looking back and knowing that they had a history with each other, it wouldn't have been too much of a stretch. A leap for sure, but you could see a logic. A model of sorts forming. These people were not stupid; they could see patterns and put things together. Lisa and Martin had their reservations - *understatement* - about how Daniel had dealt with the house, which led to Lisa agreeing to this meeting. "It was not the house that was evil", Crystal had said, "the house hid a doorway, then he went and opened it".

The cloud was denser now, so thick that John could not see the ceiling of the Church. It had crept slowly at first but then speeding along. A freight train of mist gathering speed. He had been watching it during the service for the past twenty minutes. It had seemed to advance and solidify quicker in the last five minutes. It was as if the cloud knew that the service was peaking, the congregation all seated, and the doors closed, now was its time.

*Time to do what?*

The cloud split in two; one half floated towards the altar, the other toward the doors. John watched the one gliding toward the Church's front, as it was easier than turning around to face the doors. Less likely to cause unwanted attention. Did that matter? *Probably not*; the bible-hugging crew were transfixed upon the service. He looked at Mary's legs, eyes on the prize, eyes on the prize. More people had noticed it now; a few of them pointed and gawked as it gathered above the priest's head. Their voices were quiet and uneven as they whispered to one another. It just floated for a moment, hovering above him, *waiting*, the Priest in a world of his own, reading aloud from memory.

*For one show only, a modern retelling, the gospel of the damned, just*
*you wait, it's a killer.*

The Priest was suddenly aware that his flock were not looking at him but instead looked above him. Something drawing their eyes away from him. Looking above him. He looked up and saw the cloud that had formed. The cloud darted into his open mouth. It had moved slowly before, now it moved at speed, forcibly being consumed by its unwilling host. He didn't even have time for an *Amen*. The cloud was absorbed completely, and the priests head dropped. He was looking at the floor. He lifted his head, his flock... his sheep, a thin grin formed on his lips as he looked them over.

Daniel sat alone in the bar, drinking early, alone, and hard. It had started with a single vodka, then a double and now it was going to head for triples. This was his problem, the relief of the nightmares stopping, the release from the endless terrors now needed to be filled with something else. He was an empty vessel that needed to be filled. For now, alcohol would have to suffice. In the past, it had been Lisa or his job that had helped, now he had nothing. Nothing except for the vodka and coke in the glass. The vodka's measures had risen, and the amount of coke had lowered. Daniel took a sip, brown vodka with a hint of cola. It'd do for now. Sip? Bollocks, he necked it in one and ordered another. Day drinking, never a good thing. He threw the money onto the bar, just grabbing a handful from his pocket. He used his finger, counting out the pounds and change for the drink. Once done, he took the rest and pushed it back into his pocket. He needed a piss, and now that the thought had entered his head, he needed it quickly. Standing, or alternatively wobbling, he waddled from the stool towards the toilets.

John suddenly felt on edge. It was not the cloud vanishing into the Priest as we may have expected; it was the smile that had followed. Pencil thin and straight. It was hard to describe it as a smile, but that was what it was. He had visions of guards at Aushwitz, standing with similar smiles as victims were marched towards gas chambers, never to be heard from again. This was the smile of those who enjoyed it. This was the smile of death and evil, a smile of absolute human horror.

The glazed eyes looked everywhere but settled on nothing. They seemed to focus on things that were not there. It was like they were seeing the world for the first time. He placed his arm to his side and held Mary's hand; her palm was damp from sweat. He did not have to ask; he just knew that she felt it too. The emptiness that had engulfed the Church and its congregation. He got to his feet, trying to be both quick about it and to remain as unnoticed as possible. He pulled Mary up, "What if it's from God?" she asked.

"Do you feel any goodness from him?" John replied, knowing the answer. She did not respond, and they shuffled along the pew and headed for the aisle in the centre. Excusing themselves as they passed others in the congregation, others who had yet to work out that something was wrong or were confused and unsure of what to do. Their befuddled brains trying to take it all in and make sense of what they were seeing.

They both made their way towards the door, and John could see the two ladies standing there. He realised now why the cloud had split; he understands that they will not be leaving. His heart plummeting from the earthly centre towards the depths of hell. Mrs Cartright and Miss Andrews stood at the door; the same flimsy smile decorated their lips. Mary had drawn ahead as he had slowed. It was not a lot, maybe one step, but it meant that they focused their attention on her.

Miss Andrews sprang forward and took Mary by the head, one hand on either side. She pulled Mary toward her and smacked lips with her. John stopped, startled; this was not what he had expected. This was a kiss full of passion, a full-throated teenage snog, last night of the prom, and then we will kiss. Just as suddenly as it had started, the kissing stopped. A tangoing of tongues in the dark, damp nightclub of the mouth. Mary stood with her back to him, hands slumped to her side. She turned, and he realised what had happened. Mary stood dead-eyed and looked at him, a slip of a smile starting to form on her lips. A white scar of lips pointing slightly upwards at either end.

"Shove your head up your arse" was not, it had to be said, the best of insults. It was, however, the best that Daniel could manage in his intoxicated state. Did the guy who he had shouted it at deserve to be insulted? *No*. Had Daniel earned the bloody nose and fat lip? *Undoubtedly, yes*. The punch came quick and fast; it would have been unavoidable even had Daniel had been sober, as he was drunk, he stood no chance. He felt his nose explode, blood spraying over the door and fruit machine. Daniel turned, not through choice. That was just the way his body moved from the punch and because of the drink. The second punch landed with a crunch on the side of his face depositing blood on the jukebox this time.

Lip smashed against teeth, teeth buckled but staying put, *just*. The barman was already on the phone; he had seen this play out too many times in the past. Nine-nine-nine dialled, and he was now speaking to the local coppers. Yes, they will send someone quickly. They have someone in the area. He'd heard that before. Government crackdowns, pub violence, get priority. He'd believe it when he saw it. Daniel felt the bile rising before it finally escaped, decorating the man, fruit machine and toilet doors in a slimy acidic goop. This smell would linger for longer than his fluids. Daniel slumped to the floor sitting in his own blood and vomit. The warmth of the liquids soaking through his trousers. He still had not made it to the toilet. His bladder had held on for now. He looked at his watch. The hour hand jiggled and blurred somewhere between one and two. What was he doing drinking at this time of the day! The barman walked over to Daniel, his attacker having departed the scene quickly. What had caused it? Daniel had thought he had heard the guy say something. The oldest and stupidest reason in the book. Topped only by, well, they looked at me funny.

The barman grabbed Daniel and pulled him to his feet, not saying a word as he did so. The ritual may have been new to Daniel, but it was well known to the barman. With a little bit of pulling, a lot of leading, and a dash of pushing, the barman got Daniel outside and sat him down on a bench. "What the fuck has gotten into you?" he asked, "You are usually so placid". Daniel tried to reply, but he only managed to gurgle and mumble. Is it because of the lip, nose and nausea? Or because of the drink? Maybe a little of both. A lot of it was down to the embarrassment. A car pulled up, and a man got out. He headed to the barman. "Is this him?" he asked.

"Yeah, this is him", the barman replied, shocked that the police had arrived quickly. Now he had seen it, he was still not sure he believed it. "Pressing charges?" the Policeman asked. Daniel had by now worked out that it was a policeman, his mind working at the speed of a slow snail. "No, not this time. This one, well, he is usually okay. I thought it would escalate into something more; otherwise, I wouldn't have bothered calling", the barman replied.

Daniel let out a sigh. He thought he was going to be deep in the shit. "I'll let him sleep it off", the Policeman said as he lifted Daniel from the bench and headed towards his car. "He'll probably need a piss", the barman said as they walked away. The Policeman grabbed the newspaper from the front of the car and spread it out on the rear seat as he left Daniel leaning against the car. Precariously balanced between the car door and the pavement. "You piss in my car, and we'll be having words", the Policeman said to Daniel.

"Name?" Daniel spluttered. It was all he could manage.

"That's usually my line", the Policeman said as he bundled Daniel into
the car.

"Daniel", he said finally, "Daniel James".

"Well Daniel, I'm David, David Rogers, and I'll be your ride, so I suppose you should tell me where you live". Daniel let out a sigh, things were looking up, and he answered the question. It could have been far worse.

John looked around the Church. He could see others kissing and embracing each other at random. Sometimes he could see the smoke drifting from one person to another. Floating between mouths, ears, and any other orifice. Some people were getting physical; others would watch and stimulated themselves. An infection ran rampant through the crowd, a madness spread from one to the next. The worlds worse STD running amok. John looked to the Priest. He hoped to see a moment of sanity, something to give him hope from this supposed man of God. His faith would protect him, *wouldn't it*? The Priest stood with his trousers around his ankles, penis in hand. The cilice around his leg throbbing and blood dripped downwards towards his feet. He was jerking himself as he watched the group, never taking his eyes from them; his flock was in full swing. *Say hallelujah as we fuck for the lord. Praise Jesus and cum together.*

John looked away from the Priest; he had seen enough; he had seen too much! He looked for Mary among the crowd. He spotted her; she was still near the door along with the other woman, Miss Andrews. They were working their way through people, kissing some, contaminating them with the cloud that expelled itself from their mouths. The seed of the darkness that lurked within them all, being passed to the next and then the next. Soon they would all be infected. Poisoned by the evil, corrupted by the sin, did he have any chance to escape? Could he save Mary? His question was answered almost as quickly as it had been thought. He felt it at first, a punch into the small of his back. It was like being jabbed by an uppercut into his lower back... a strong punch low down from someone who had the strength of an adult. John tried to look at what had hit him and realised that he could not bend quite far enough. Whatever it was had been stuck in that place on his back that you just can't see. He ran his hands to where he had felt the blow. He could feel the warmth at first and then the dampness. He pulled his hand forward and looked at the blood that had gathered. He was bleeding and bleeding badly. He reached back around, feeling for what was still stuck in him, long and thin, but not a knife. It felt wooden. He could feel the grooving on the wood. John grasped at it, paused for a moment, thinking if it is wise to remove it; he decided to pull, and as he did so, he felt the pain rocketed from the spot. Pain thundered through him. Starting at the small of his back, and reverberated upwards and downwards through his body. Hitting his feet and head at the same time as it shot through him. He fell to his knees, forgetting the object he had pulled for a moment; he dropped it to the floor.

John knelt. He looked like a man at prayer as he glanced around. Looking for the thing that had been in his back. It was a crucifix. He had been felled by the symbol of this religion. The son of God, hanging from the crucifix, leading him away from this life. Blood soaked into the unvarnished wood. He looked up at everyone in the Church, one last chance, one final hope. He saw Mary coming towards him, she was going to save him, he was sure of that.
*Mary, my Mary! Help me.*

Mary got to him, and she kicked her heels off, those heels that both she and he adored. She now stood three inches shorter. She picked them up and held them in her hand. Holding them by the toes rather than her usual finger in the heel. Her Church shoes. She stood and looked at him, John on his knees and her standing before him. The opposite of their usual post-church routine. She whipped one of her shoes at his face; the heel punctured his cheek, *penetrating him.*

It slipped through the soft skin as quickly as her heels would do were it a grassy lawn. She ripped it back from his face, his mouth filled with blood and air. Mary bought the other shoe up, slamming it into the other side of his face. His other cheek was torn open as she ripped it away. A massive gash along the sides of his face. There was an unnatural strength about her; she was being driven by insanity. The madwoman had taken the wheel, and she was not letting go. The blood in his mouth sprayed outwards, covering the floor beside him. A human sprinkler of blood. He fell to the side, and she jumped upon him, pinning his arms on either side with her stockinged legs. He looked at her, pleading with his eyes; *no, don't,* he begged. She was the more dominant one, nobody would have ever guessed that, and this time, as always, she would take what she wanted.

Mary looked forward above and ahead of John. He couldn't help himself; He had to know what she was looking at. He arched his head back so that he could see. The pain crashed through him as he did so. His cheeks ripping slightly as the skin tightened. The Priest was heading toward them. He watched the Priest, who was still jerking and working. Mary lowered herself, bringing herself to her knees; she lowered herself onto his face. She was careful, methodical even, to make sure his arms could not get free. She had him pinned by the knees as she lowered. He tried to scream, but the screams were muffled, muffled by his Mary. He felt the Priest climax over him, darkness suffocating him as his lover sat on his face, wetness from the Priest over his shirt. John thought it was all over, then he felt Mary thrusting, and as she pushed, the heel was bought down once more as she smashed them into the top of his head. Thrusting and smashing is the last thought, the feeling that he died with, pounding and thrusting from the woman he loves.

    Mrs Cartright had left the *party. She* had wanted to stay, wanted to play with the others, but she had other plans. She had left the front of the church, walked the aisle, and headed for the kitchen in the rear. She knew what she wanted was back there; she just had to find it. The Church had an old generator as a backup for power outages. It was from the days when people would gather at a church in times of need. If it had a generator, it had to also have fuel. She had seen it once before when working in the kitchen, she just could not remember where! She pulled boxes from the shelves throwing them behind, disregarding anything that was not inflammable or a liquid. Boxes and paperwork were flung across the room, scattering themselves everywhere. She finally found what she was looking for. Five litres, it may not be enough, but it would have to do.

    Mrs Cartright tapped the edge of the drum; it gave a satisfying full knock, no echo here, it was full or near as damn it. She dragged the drum into the nave. It would become lighter the more that she poured. She started with the altar, just enough here and made her way into the crowd of people that had gathered.

Pouring petrol over each and every one as she went. They did not stop what they are doing. They continued the acts, some carnal, some vicious, many both. Some jerking, all working and all smirking. She covered every person that she could see and then stood in the centre of them all. The can was light enough for her now. She held it above her head and poured what remained over her body and that of the people around her. The fuel dripping down her head and covering her and them. She reached into one of her pockets and pulled out a packet of cigarettes and a box of matches. She placed a cigarette in her mouth and threw the rest of the packet to the floor. Discarding it with the fornicating mass. She lit the matchstick, held it to the cigarette and puffed away at it, taking a drag as she dropped the lit match.

    The flames danced in all directions as the lit matchstick hit the ground. A jaunted dance of flames and bodies, not one person made a run for it, not one stopped even if the person they were with had died and was burning.
Necrophilia early afternoon running rampant and wild in this Church. The fire crawled the walls, and smoke filled the Church. Mrs Cartright just stood in the centre of it all, not making a noise, not moving, just watching. A giant human wick in the centre of a flaming orgy of sexual wax. When the flames snaked up to her eyes, they popped from the heat. The clear fluids from inside them flowed down her cheeks. Bubbling to the bottom of her face and then

dripping to the crowd. She dropped to her knees in the fire and then lay in it. She blindly welcomed its warm embrace.

    The cloud drifted from a window that had shattered in the heat. It mixed with the smoke from the fire. Nobody noticed it as it sailed ever higher. As it wafted away from the Church.

# The Descent

The cloud, *our outcasts*, just waited and watched from afar. The Church had been *fun*. The Church had been *excellent*! Like any of us, it was still learning; it would always be learning. Growing not just in numbers but also in strength and intelligence. It needed something. It wanted to have more fun. It had found something it enjoyed, something that fulfilled it. And, it wanted more. It hovered near a department store, looking and waiting for something to take its fancy; it did not take long.

Daniel sat alone at home. He had napped and slept the drinking off. The afternoon sun starting to droop from the sky. His head was banging. Playing the greatest hits of every classic rock band all at once. Thankfully he had not spent more time at the police station. The Policeman had been a decent sort and bought him home. His hangover...

*Had enough of Jailhouse Rock? Well, here is Folsum Prison Blues;*
*wait, The Hurricane is in the queue. We have all your favourites.*

Daniel stumbled from the sofa he had slept on, using a hand to steady himself as he rose. He needed drugs, lots of drugs.

He staggered up the stairs, one step at a time and slowly, and headed to the bathroom. He opened the cabinet above the sink and saw the pills, his collection of painkillers. He bought a box almost every time he visited the supermarket. Why did they have to be in packs of sixteen? He did not usually need them because of drinking. It was the nightmares that gave him headaches. That was why he had the collection. He popped two pills from one box and two from another. He knew that you were supposed to take them two hours apart, but he didn't care, not today. He dry swallowed the four pills and headed for the toilet.

David looked at the Church doors, what was left of them, and walked inside. The Church had only just been given the all-clear from the fire department. "There is some fucked up shit in there", he had been told. Nothing they had said, nor anything they could have said, could have prepared him for what awaited. David walked inside and looked over the scene. A few firefighters were still there sifting through the mess. They were checking or any embers they had missed. "Jesus Christ", David muttered to himself, the son of God fast becoming his go-to curse. Many of the bodies lay in a charred heap in the centre of the aisle. They had - *it appeared* - crawled to the fire and tried to gather as close to it as they could. Water dripped from everything to the floor.

*Drip, drip, drip...*

David looked over what remained of the wooden pews. He saw people sat on each other, mounted and burnt together. Held in place by the remains of the fire. Skin merging with their partner's skin to form one shape. The crafting clay of life burnt into one human-like figure.

"Believe it or not, but they were shagging", the firefighter said.

"Shagging? During this?" David replied, with a note of astonishment ringing in his voice. A hint of the report he had read fluttering in the brain waves like a butterfly at play. "Yep, as far as I can see, they kept on fucking while the fire raged". David shook his head, unbelievable; *why*? "Okay, tell me what happened", David asked the firefighter.

Daniel sat at the kitchen table with a coffee in hand. The radio was on in the background, only now the volume was lower than usual. He took a sip from the cup as the news rolled in.

*The fire at Our Lady & The English Martyrs' Church has been extinguished. The police and firefighters are now on the scene. Reports are coming in suggesting that the fire was a deliberate act, and so far, everyone is thought to have died. The local Priest "John Westly" is believed to have perished along with his congregation. If you have any information or think you may have had family involved in this, please call.........*

Daniel turned the radio off and finished his coffee.

*Depressing, what was the world coming to? Christ, a Church as well!*

As if he was being answered by a God. God giving him a tinkle to tell him precisely what the world was coming to, the phone in the hallway started to ring. Daniel got up and headed down the hallway. He was steadier now on his feet. The coffee and pills had begun to do the job. He looked at the phone as if it was an alien object, it rang, and he knew what to do; it was just that nobody called on the landline these days. He picked up the phone and said, "Hello".

The cloud hung in the air. It kept itself high enough to not be noticed but close enough so that it could see. This could be perfect, but could it pull it off? The doll had been hard work, more of a challenge than it had expected, but it had worked. This would be similar; it was just bigger. It watched the shop window and bided its time. The cloud dropped lower, heading toward the shop. It thinned itself as it did so. When it has reached the ground, it was nothing but a slight fog. It approached the door and made its way inside. It could have possessed a human, but where, it thought, was the fun in that?

"A psychic called Crystal? I am not having that", Daniel said as he spoke on the phone.

"I think she is genuine. At the very least, she is engaging and knows things that she shouldn't", Martin replied. Martin understood Daniel's scepticism; they were all sceptical of psychics. It was part of the job. They had met far too many charlatans and not enough genuine ones. "You think she is real?" Daniel questioned. Martin hesitated for just a moment before he replied. "I think she is trustworthy. Do I think she is psychic? I don't know... She could be, she may not be. I do think that we should listen to her and hear her out".

"Okay, I will head over to the office. I'll be there in half an hour".

"What makes something like this happen?" David asked the firefighter.

"That is your job, mate; mine is to tell you how. Yours is to find out why". David grunted at this, the firefighter was right, but he could have used any help he could have got with this one. "I just can't wrap my head around this one", he said. "It can't be drugs, can it?" David looked around, hopelessly looking for a sign of drug use.

"I have not seen anything unusual", the firefighter said. He glanced around the smouldering remains, "Nothing that indicates drugs use, *unusual*... Yeah, I've seen that". David shuffled his feet, trying to avoid standing on something that could give him a clue as to why.

*Unusual, yes, that is one way to describe things.*

The cloud studied it, and if it could have, it would have smiled. It was perfect. The colour was the best bit, white and pure, everything that it was not. It slipped inside, contaminating the plastic, much like it had the doll. It was stronger now, but with strength came an awareness. It was aware of the one who had set it free, and it came to understand that he could also banish it. How did it come across this information? It did not know; it had just come to it. A voice drifting through the mist that formed its being warned him of this man.
Tentatively it tried to lift an arm, the arm raised, and it felt control. This time it had the power; it had an ability that came from the other's strength, power in numbers.

Daniel paid for the taxi and went to the office. His head was still pounding, but now it was a mild drumbeat. The slow tapping of a jazz track before it hits its timing. The incessant wittering from the taxi driver should have made it worse, but thankfully, it had not. He could live with that; he would have to live with that. Daniel opened the door and headed inside the Institute.

*Psychic? Bah.*

The office was the same as always; only three people were waiting for him instead of two. Crystal was sitting in the spare chair, *in his chair*, sipping at a cup of tea. If she noticed him entering the room, she doesn't show it. She just sat and drank her tea. Absorbed in her own thoughts.

Crystal, however, had seen Daniel enter, and she was not really paying much attention to her tea either. The thing she was paying attention to. The thing that was sapping all of her awareness was the feeling in her mind. She had tightness and a sense of unease; something was going to happen. Something
was happening! She kept trying to see, trying to visualise the threat that she felt. There is a car, but the driver, she cannot make out the driver. The driver was wrong. The driver was something she has not felt before.

The woman shrieked as it had walked from the department store.

Strolling like any normal human being. It did not bother it. It liked the attention, and it enjoyed the screams.

*Let them scream, let them panic. Let them all fear me.*

The plastic had creaked and squeaked at first. Straining as it was forced to move in ways that it had never been designed to do, but soon it moved freely enough. It had laboured at first, and it had wondered if it was strong enough for this. The plastic, though, had soon given up its fight. The car was another problem and was easily solved. It looked through its group of outcasts; it had what it needed somewhere. It did. A man among them had experience with cars, someone who could do what needed to be done.

Daniel looked at Crystal. Her eyes crossed the room to where he stood. Finally, she seemed to acknowledge him, "Oh, hi" was all that she said. He looked at her, and the first word that popped into his head was *scatty*. She looked like the type of person who would put the cereal into the fridge, then the milk into the cupboard. He then imagined that she would sit down to work, then something else would enter her mind, and she would be off to do that. She dressed in the stereotype of a fortune teller, with a long flowing dress and a loose-fitting top. Crystal looked at him and just thought, *cynic*. They both knew the phrase that you should never judge a book by its cover; they had both ignored that advice.

Something then happened, a thing that it had not expected, something that it could not have foreseen. The plastic smashed as it punched into the ignition, plastic upon plastic, both gave. Plastic started to fall to the well of the car. Some from the dashboard and some from its moulded *hand*. It watched as it fell, cursing itself for not thinking. Wishing that it had been more considered in its approach to this new fragile body. The plastic that had broken from it stopped in mid-air and just floated between the well and the dashboard. Tendrils of smoke drifted from the breaks in both its hand and the falling pieces. Cloud mixed with plastic, plastic mixed with the cloud. The broken pieces started to float back toward the hand, drawn back to the host by the hazy mist. The fractured pieces hovered back to the body, nestling in place almost entirely, with only the thinnest of fog showing the cracks. It instinctively raised the hand to look at it. It was something it did not need to do, but having a head - *of sorts* - made it revert to old habits. It clenched the fist, good as new. The fingers even bent more easily now it had been broken. It pulled the wires from the dashboard and follows the instructions that it had been given by the thief.

Betty Davies walked along the pavement, not quite sure if she could believe her own eyes. Bets, as she was known to her friends, Betty to many and Mrs Davies to those that she did not like, she could be a fierce woman. She was not one to suffer fools gladly, nor did she have any qualms about speaking her mind. Had someone told her that they had seen what she had just seen, she'd have thought them crazy. This had made her pause and consider. She first thought that it must have been kids playing a joke, but then it had moved. There was something in the way that it looked at the hand that had made her stop. She watched as it examined its hand. Steam surrounded the hand, lifting from it like the vapour rising from a pipe on a cold winters morning. It had made a fist and then stared at it. It was then that she had decided what she would do. Betty had rounded the corner. The Police station was minutes away.

"I am not special", Crystal said; she held the cup tightly in her hands.

"Then, how do you know all about this" Daniel demanded to know. He slammed his hands into his lap when she just shook her head. "I don't know", Crystal said, "It's just me. It is what I am and what I do. It is nothing special when you have been doing it your whole life". She finished this breathless sentence and put the cup down on the desk. "Yes, but how can..." Daniel was cut off by Lisa. She held her hand in the air to stop him mid-flow. "I think we need to start again" Lisa looked at Daniel, "Calmly this time", she finished.
"Crystal, start again. What do you know?" Martin asked.

"Well..." Crystal said.

Betty entered the Police station and approached the desk. It was an old fashioned local - *in a loose sense* - station and had yet to have a security screen put up around the desk. It will come in time, she thought, well, if they don't close the place first. One minute they are banging on about law and order, the next? Closing police stations and courts. She rang the small bell that sat on the desk and waited.

The engine revved wildly. The *foot* pressed down on the accelerator, lifted for a second and then pushed down again. The car jumping as it pushed its foot down; it wanted to be free. It moved its hand down to the gearstick and shifted it into first. The memories coming back immediately, the lessons it had learnt in life coming back to it, coming back quick and fast.

Crystal knew about everything; in total, she knew far more than they knew. She had told them of the house, how she had felt Daniel there. She had no idea who he was at the time and that the feeling that she had felt was not unusual. Then it went quiet. She didn't know why, but Daniel did. I was in the hospital, he thought to himself. "Then you burnt the house down", Crystal said and eyed Daniel.

"Hello, how can I help?" The Policewoman asked as she arrived at the desk. Betty looked at her and then started to question herself, how was she going to report this? "Well", she said, "I saw someone breaking into a car". "Okay, Madam", the Policewoman said. Oh, how Betty hated being called Madam. "Can you tell me your name, please?"

"Mrs Davies", Betty replied sharply.

It turned the steering wheel and applied a slight push to the accelerator. The car edged forward from the parking space. It hit the car parked just in front, no harm, it thought as it slid forward, leaving a scratch along the side. It turned onto the straight. *More manageable*, it pushed the accelerator down. So what if it crashed? It thought. It isn't going to hurt me. The car sped onwards.

"But don't you see?" Crystal asked, stressing the final word. "The house was left to you so that you'd investigate it and hopefully understand what is there".

"And you burned it down", Martin added with a sigh. "I knew it was too easy".

"Then there was the car thief", Crystal said. "Then it moved to the family".

"So your saying you think these things are connected?" Daniel asked. Crystal looked at him again before she continued. "Then it was the Church today. It burnt all those poor people".

"But, you couldn't go to the police?" Lisa asked. The moment the words had slipped from her mouth; she knew it was a stupid question. "Hello, I'm psychic, and I have information. Think it over, sis", Martin said. Crystal had not taken her eyes from Daniel,

"And no", she said. "I don't think these things were linked; I know they were".

"Well, it must have been kids, or well at least a kid", Betty said as she started to doubt what she had seen. "And why do you say that?" The Policewoman asked. This was the part that Betty was not looking forward to. How would she go about explaining what she had seen? "He was in fancy dress", Betty said. "Dressed as a mannequin", she added, trying to make it sound like an afterthought or an irrelevance. "A mannequin?" The Policewoman said, surprised. She'd heard many things in her short time working here, but this was a new one. She raised an eyebrow as she did it. "Yes!" Betty said, "I know what it sounds like, but just around the corner outside of M&S, I saw them trying to steal a car".

"It is happening again. I can feel it", Crystal said. She held her hands to her head as if trying to push the thoughts back inside. Pushing the palms to her temples. "It is in a car. I can feel the movement".

"How can it drive?" Daniel asked. His scepticism subsided a little, but it was always ready to charge back to the front. "I don't know. I think it has taken someone or something. I just see a cloud".

"Okay, so where is it", Martin asked her.

"I can't tell. It is all moving too fast", Crystal said. "I can only tell you that it is happening right now!"

The Policewoman watched as Mrs Davies left the station. Dotty old bat. *And yes, Sir, that is my professional opinion*, she thought to herself, probably just looking for attention. The Policewoman pushed the notes to one side. Still, she would fill in the forms. Dot the i's and cross the t's as she was always taught. She was filling out the paperwork when she heard the screeching of tyres. Looking up from the desk, she could see the old lady outside. Mrs Davies had turned to her left, her jaw dropped in horror. She just stared at the noise that they had both heard.

The tyres screamed, and the breaks squealed; it didn't care. It did not give a shite, not that it could. It needed something done, and it would do it. It would not hold back on a bit of fun. Why should it? It saw the old lady and took only seconds to decide; the car swerved and hit the lady head-on. Her legs smashed into the bumper; they were almost ripped in half. Her head rebounded off the bonnet and then smashed into the windscreen, splintering the glass. The mannequin behind the wheel punched the glass, hitting it with anger and supernatural strength. The body bounced from the window as it struck, the plastic hand shattering again and re-joining through its misty veins. The body fell from the car; the head being smashed by the rear wheel. The sound of the breaking bones reverberated down the narrow street; it bounced from building to building.

The Policewoman stood with her mouth open and gawked at the scene. She had seen the car hit the woman, then she had seen inside. Finally, she had watched as the vehicle had jumped six inches in the air at the rear. She had no idea why at first; she then saw the aftermath and the woman's body, the head smashed into the ground. Another Policeman came running into the reception area, "What the hell was that?" He asked.

"Someone..." she stopped, trying to pull herself together. "Someone dressed as a mannequin just hit that old lady with a car", she said with a stutter.

And the car continued to speed on down the street, heading towards the Institute.

# The Chase

The car powered down the street. Its wheels shrieked at every twist and turn. It had taken only four people to cause the car to cry out in pain. It was an older model, but still, it was not made for hit and runs.

The first had been the old woman, a needless one but fun nonetheless. That had damaged the windscreen, point one to the human body. The second and third had been a young couple holding hands, very much in love and just strolling the pathway together. It had taken this one slowly, not wanting to cause further damage to the windscreen. It had crept up behind them, sneaking as quietly as it could in a vehicle. When it felt that it was as close as it would get, it honked the horn, startling the couple. They both jumped in unison, span and looked at the car with the mannequin in the driver's seat. They did not have time to react as the car lunged at them, hitting them within seconds. It then braked, slammed the car into reverse and backed up a little. It watched as they crawled closer to each other, still hand in hand. Legs crippled from the violence and force of the bumper, they looked on with desperation in their eyes. Then it started to move once more, very slowly now. The bones crunched as the car rolled over them. It was slow enough to enjoy the feeling but too quick for them to have escaped. It didn't look behind once it continued on its way. It knew the bodies were being dragged. It could hear the scraping; *it needn't look.* It was not though the bodies scraping as it had thought. It was, in fact, the exhaust. Points two and three to the humans, it was now that it stopped counting. The noise rocketed as the exhaust fell from the car, dragged and pulled free by one of the bodies. There goes the element of surprise, it thought.

"I can feel it drawing closer", Crystal said with a ping of desperation in her voice. "I think it is heading here".

"Here? Why?" Lisa asked.

"Because of him", Crystal said as she pointed at Daniel. Her finger shook in the air. She was scared. "It thinks that you can stop it", she said. "So, it plans to kill you". Daniel stood in the corner, still unsure if he trusted Crystal.
"Why me?" he asked her.

"It thinks that you are somehow the one who can kill it", she answered
without missing a beat.

"But how?" Martin said.

It turned the corner, closer now. The sirens in the background were growing increasingly louder. The carnage, as well as the deaths, it had left behind keeping them busy. That would not last once they called for backup. The fourth person it had hit had been an accident. It would have never stood up in any court, of course.

*The first three were just for fun! The fourth, well, I didn't mean that one.*

Not that you could have ever taken a cloud, a fog of supernatural mist to court, but still, it mattered to it. It did not know why; it should not have mattered, but it did. It was the speed that had done it. The voice deep inside telling it that this was not the game it wanted. As it rounded the corner, the old man had just been there. Old, frail and skin and bones, he had popped as the car had hit him. He exploded like a blood-filled water balloon being dropped from a height—blood, brains, bone, and old man goo splattering all over the front of the car. None of this was a problem. The fact it had killed him accidentally and was bothered by it quickly subsided into anger when it realised what had happened to the car. The old fools stick, his damned walking stick, had got jammed somehow and into the bonnet of the vehicle. The bonnet flipped open like a muppets mouth, the roar of the exhaust screaming along with it. The blood was soon cleared with wipers and washers. Something just felt wrong about the man. It felt that he was not part of a design. He was not part of the clouds game. It pushed the thought away and continued.

Crystal had started to get visibly agitated. She chewed on the end of her fingernails and shifted in her seat as the others talked. "We have to go", she finally snapped. "It'll be fine", Lisa said. "Nobody is coming here". She sounded sure and confident. Daniel was starting to have his doubts. "Maybe we should go elsewhere", he said, trying to hide the worry in his voice.

"You okay?" Martin inquired. He had, over the years, seen Daniel in plenty of different moods; this was a new one. "I'm fine", he lied. "I just think that it is better safe than sorry". The thought of all this lingered. He felt that he was the star player, the important one, but did not know how to play or why he was playing. "Thank you", Crystal said. "You've made the right choice, maybe for the wrong reasons, but it is the right choice". Couldn't she have just left it at *thank you*, Daniel mused.

It turned the final corner, and it could see the Institute up ahead. It had not expected to see the four people leaving the building getting into a bright red car. The exhaust bellowed and roared as it pushed its foot down. The bonnet flapped like an open mouth singing a one-off petrol-fuelled opera. It galloped down the street, singing its tune, screaming its guttural message for all to hear.

Daniel looked over his shoulder as he bundled himself into the back seat. He looked at the car hurtling down the road towards them. He glanced quickly to check all of them were in the car; they were. "Drive, fucking drive", he shouted to Lisa. Lisa almost fumbled the keys, but she didn't. She turned the key, and the Cosworth came to life. The other car had roared; the Cosworth had a finely tuned engine that hummed like the baseline in an old rock classic. Lisa floored it. The front wheel's span, and then the car took off.

It had to turn at the last minute as the red car sped away. It did not think it would make it at first, but it did. The red car was fast, faster than it could have imagined, but it kept pace, *just*. The punk screaming after the tuned classic rock star, blaring the music they made for all to hear. Demanding to be heard.

Hit and run? Mannequin?? Stolen car??? David opened his sandwich as he answered the radio call. Driving from the garage as he took his first bite. He was moving quickly but not speeding. He wanted to get there in one piece and, he wanted to finish his sandwich. It had been a long day. The traffic lights were green; *damn*, he sailed through while taking another mouthful.

"Can't you go any faster?" Martin asked with worry in his voice. The other car had gained on them. It was driven without caution. "I could, but I won't", Lisa shot back promptly. "I drive safely, not quickly". They flew around the next corner, the car gripping the ground like it was on a magnetic scalextric strip. Lisa dodged the slowly moving traffic as she pushed forwards. "You bought a Cosworth to drive slowly?" Crystal asked, unaware that this was a discussion that Lisa and Daniel had been over many times. "Slowly, no, not always", Lisa said, turning the wheel left sharply. The car skidded around the corner; the mirror on the side clipped a van as if proving a point. "Safely, yes", Lisa finished as she jammed the car up a gear, ramming it between third and fourth. Lisa looked at the broken mirror and cursed under a breath as she saw the car behind.

> It was not gaining on them, but it was not losing much ground either.

They had the advantage of speed and cornering, but it had the weight advantage and the benefit of not giving a fuck. The bonnet had been blown off in a gust of wind, flipping over the roof of the car, and the windscreen knocked out, and the only passenger a hollow shop mannequin. The red wing mirror flew through the air and bounced on the front of its car, bounced and then fell into the engine cavity. The car swerved and slid along the side of another. It banged its hand against the steering wheel as the Escorts part settled on the air filter, cursing the traffic.

David had spotted them and was following from a distance. He was trying to catch them but also to think one step ahead. He had an idea that they were headed for the seafront. "Not good, not good at all", David said to himself. He knew something that the driver of the red Escort was only just learning. He knew that the driver of the pursuing car didn't have any problem with driving into people. He even had the feeling that the person enjoyed doing just that. Why else would they have hit so many people? He swerved a few cars as he approached the roads to the seafront with caution.

"Head to the seafront", Daniel said. "It's straight. We can outpace them
on it".

"Where do you think I was heading?" Lisa asked. Not a note of emotion in her voice; she was concentrating on the drive. Lisa shifted down to take the next corner, then back up as they hit a straight. Brake slightly, clutch, shift clutch and flooring it; it was almost one smooth motion. She zigzagged between cars, thankful for the wide road. The other car came crashing around the corner after them. Grinding its way along the row of vehicles that had been parked there. Missing some cars by mere millimetres. They could see the sea in front of them now, they only had one more corner, and then they were on the straight.
They had to only hope that it was not too busy.

David had turned off the road and headed to the high street. If he was right, he *might* stand a chance; *if* he was right... The high street ran parallel to the seafront, but what it had were intersecting roads. If he could make it to one of them before they did. He could cut them off. David flicked the switch and turned the siren and lights on, and this time, he drove fast. He looked to his right as he took the first crossing at speed, banging the car over the speed hump. He looked to his right and saw the red flash of the other car passing at the same time. They had made the seafront. The cars in front of him moved out of the way as he sped past.

"And when we run out of seafront?" Martin asked. Lisa touched the brakes, just a touch to slow them down the tiniest amount so that when she did what she needed to do next, she felt safe. It was only a second, but she shot him a look. It was the type of look that people talked about in bars up and down the country. *And when they gave me the look, then I knew I was in the shit*, The barflies whispered. Others would nod along in agreement. *Oh aye, I know that look*, they would murmur before taking another mouthful of ale. Martin had been lucky enough to never have had a partner who could pull the look off. He now knew how others felt. *He knew how the other half lived*. He now knew that feeling that you get in the pit of your stomach, not butterflies but pterodactyls. "Point taken", he said. Promising himself that he would never again ask Lisa a question like that when she was driving. The other car almost shunted them from behind in that second. Lisa had accelerated once more, the RS engine humming as it was let free, and that was all that had saved them from a bump in the rear.

David was flying, almost literally. The car felt like it was being thrown about as it bounced between speedbumps. He was ahead of them, *not by much*, but he was leading. He had to hope his luck held as he slowed for the corner. If the road was clear, he would speed down it and get out in front. If it wasn't? That would be game over for him. He'd never catch them again. David pushed the brakes, and the car decelerated, just enough to take the corner and stop if needed. He was a Policeman at the end of the day. He turned right, looked, and the road was clear. David pushed his hand down to his side, checking the seat belt. *Do or die*, he thought as he pushed the accelerator down.

It had hit the brakes suddenly as the car in front had done so. It was not what it had wanted to do. It was not what it should have done, but it was what it had done. Was it an instinct left over from its human mind? A remnant from its distant past? Why had the other car braked? It did not know about the look that Lisa was giving Martin, *knew of the look*, but not about this particular one. It also did not know about David, who right at this moment was driving down the side street. What it did know was that the metal red wing mirror that had held stubbornly onto the air filter now jumped forward toward the front of the car, as the car had jolted.

The mirror jumped down and jammed itself into the front radiator, damaging it in the process. It cursed itself for braking, cursed the mirror for moving and then cursed the radiator for springing a leak. Hot jets of steam rose into the air. This car would be dead and dead soon.

Lisa, Martin, Crystal and Daniel didn't know what they would do when the road ended at the yacht club that they were fast approaching. David had no idea that the two cars were almost joined together, a tandem of cars. Crystal saw the blue flash in the side street first. She nudged Daniel and pointed to it.
"Finally, some help", Daniel said. Martin looked over, Lisa her eyes pinned to the road skipping past cars and hoping that nobody walked out unaware as the road narrowed. She hammered the horn almost continuously.

They shot past like a bullet just as the nose of David's car poked out of the street. Martin, Crystal and Daniel saw David and David saw them. David also saw what was about to happen, and he braced just in time. The front of David's car clipped the back of the pursuing vehicle. Metal screamed, steel screeched, and the plastic cracked as the cars did the scrapheap samba. David's car continued forward, snipping at the end of the other. His car collided with one parked on the front, his body slamming forward with the seat belt holding him in place. The airbag exploded, cushioning his face from the full force of the blow. He still bloodied his nose on the steering wheel. He pushed himself back in the seat, and although he was not religious, he crossed his chest.

The other car span, arse end out first, rear flying to the side causing it to turn ninety degrees. As the car turned, it tried to spin the steering wheel towards the skid, trying to take back control, but it was no use. The car flipped, rising into the air, and the mannequin was thrown upwards, smashing against the roof. The car came back to the ground with a thump, metal screeching once again as it dragged against the tarmacked road. The mannequin was dumped back into the seats with a jolt. It cracked upon impact, a great big crack where its backside should have been. Crack created to imitate crack. Steam poured from the engine, rising to the heavens trying to escape. It considered its options for a moment and then decided to flee. It knew at least one in the red car was a threat. To kill them in a car was easy. Going face to face - *so to speak* - would have been a risk that it was unwilling to take at this point. *Why had it felt this way*? It was not sure. It felt like it was part of something bigger. It drifted from its plastic body and into the steam from the engine; it then floated upwards.

Lisa jammed the brakes hard, skidded and pulled the Escort to a halt. The brakes let out a sigh as smoke poured from them. She looked at the missing wing mirror and placed her hand upon the dashboard. "Sorry", she said to nobody but the car. Daniel had seen something, something that had caught his eye, and he opened the door and stepped away from the car. He ignored the twisted metal hulk that was left of the car that had been chasing them. Like the house when he had returned, it felt safe and empty now. He stole a look as he walked past, seeing only the mannequin lying dead on the front seats. He was heading for the police car, something he had noticed when glancing.

Daniel got to the police car just as the man was staggering from it. How he had survived, he would never know. Blind luck, he supposed. Daniel got over to him and placed a hand on his shoulder. "Are you okay?" He asked. David looked at Daniel, smiled, and said, "Hello again, Daniel. You sobered up quickly".

# The Aftermath

David rushed to the other car, leaving Daniel, and peered inside. "Where did they go?" He called back to Daniel. Daniel shrugged his shoulders. "No idea. I came straight to your car". It was the truth. Why mention that he had *felt* or *sensed* that the car was empty so had just glanced at it? "Copper or criminal. Figured it was best to go to the copper first", he added. The others had left the Escort and had gathered next to it. Lisa wandered around to the other car and examined the engine compartment. "Aye, that makes some sense", David said and turned to face the group. "So, do any of you want to tell me what the hell just happened?" He asked, watching each of them as he did so, looking for any reaction.

Saved by the bell, *well*, the sirens and Lisa. The sirens indicated that backup had finally arrived, as the police cars barged into the scene, and Lisa was swearing at the destroyed vehicle. Swearing like a drunken sailor on a night off. "Bastards, utter bastards. Fucking wankers", she shouted at the mess of metal, steel, and plastic. She walked back to the others holding the broken wing mirror in her hands. "Do you have any idea how much this will cost to replace!" She continued ranting as she waved the wing mirror in their faces. "Next time, we're taking your car". Martin looked at her, still wary from the earlier encounter in the car. "Had we taken mine, then it would have caught us". he said. Daniel did not bother to even reply. He knew she did not mean his 2CV. Crystal was the first one who said something that caught Davids attention. "It is gone from here, hasn't it?" David did not give anyone a chance to reply, and he moved in quickly with his question. "What do you mean it's gone?"

"That", Martin answered, "Is quite a long story".

"Oh, I have time", David said, smiling, "I have the time".

The four of them returned to the Escort and waited for David. He had headed to the Police officers that had arrived on the scene. "What do we tell him?" Daniel asked. Crystal looked up. She had been deep in thought, "The truth?" She suggested. "Jesus, he'll have us dragged to the looney bin the second we finish", Martin said unhelpfully. "I don't think we'll have much choice in the matter", Daniel said. "The second he looks any of us up, and he will, he will see what we do. The guy isn't thick".

"And", Lisa added. "We are going back to the Institute, so that is a bit of
a giveaway". Daniel shook his head, trying to think of a way out from this.

"How'd you know him anyway?" Martin asked.

"Well, I..." Daniel started before David cut him off. None of them had heard David approaching. All four had been so concerned with what they would tell him that their attention was elsewhere. "He", David said, leaning on the car and pointing at Daniel, "Was going to piss in my car. He was pissed this morning, and I picked him up". David left it dangling for a moment, always watching to see what the reaction would be. It was a gaping wide-mouthed shock from Lisa and Martin. "You were pissed? Today!" Lisa exclaimed.

"Yeah, okay. It is bad, but the chase and coffee sobered me up", Daniel defended himself. Crystal, she just looked dazed and confused. "Anyway, budge over", David said to Crystal and Daniel in the back seat. "I suppose we are going to your Institute. I will tell you all about it on the way", he finished. He has looked us up already, Martin thought. Lisa mourned the damage to her car and Daniels recklessness. Crystal considered if going to them was a good idea and how she would explain herself. Daniel thought about what a tight squeeze it was, and when David started to tell the story of how they had met, it seemed to get tighter still.

Back at the Institute, they sat down to talk. Daniel thought he would be
doing most of the talking, but Crystal was the one with something to say.

"I want you to think of the balls on a snooker table", Crystal started. "Imagine they are all the same colour, and you can't tell the difference between them". She looked the others over before continuing, "Each ball is a different universe",

"A different universe?" Daniel asked.

"Yes", Crystal replied abruptly, "Do you know the Legend of Lilith?" David just sat and listened. In his years as a Policeman, he had learnt to let people talk when they wanted to. "Bits and bobs", Martin said.

"It is nonsense", Lisa commented. Daniel had expected Crystal to argue this point, but she just seemed to accept it. "I have to agree", Daniel said finally. "It's humbug". Maybe she had become used to people dismissing her, he thought. "Maybe it is, maybe it isn't", Crystal said with a sigh. "Things get warped in time. Stories become a legend, and a legend becomes a fairy tale. Who can know for sure?" She left the question hanging before continuing. "The Lilith legend claims that she either created the other worlds or that she found a way to visit them. She would visit, wreak havoc and then leave. Marlon, Merlin, we presume, captured her and jailed her in a magic mirror".

"Hogwash, as I said", Daniel commented. "Some Princess is supposed to have freed her. Set her free using stones from the original stone that held Excalibur".

"Lilith then captures, recruits, or creates a handful of minions" Lisa took over and added a little more. "Then, she vanishes". Martin finished.

"So you do not believe it?" David asked.

"That's a tough one", Martin replied. "Do you believe in Jesus, officer?" David opened his hands and held them out. "Who can know for sure?" He answered.

"Exactly", Lisa said, butting in. "We can never know. Did Jesus exist? Maybe in some form or another. Some guy was born in the area and preached the word of what we now call Christ or God. Then it is written about, sanitised and made mythical. So is the Lilith Legend true? Parts of it are, no doubt, but much of it could be just the ramblings of an insane mind".

"See, claptrap", Daniel added, unhelpfully.

"The important thing in all of this is the cloth, the green empty between the worlds. We are all agreed that something is out there, and it is something that we each have some knowledge in dealing with. It could be anything. We have no way to know. Your Institute has been doing this far longer than I have" Crystal said this as a statement. She was taking over from the bickering about what was real and what was not. She expected them all to nod in agreement. "You will have to excuse me if I rule myself out of your little grouping", David said. Daniel let out a small laugh as he was used to being the cynic in this group. Crystal had seemed a little meek, a little distant when he had first met her. He was learning that his first impression was wrong. "Yes, well", Crystal said impatiently, "When you have been chased by a mannequin driving a car, then you may have a different view". David thought about replying and arguing the point. Chased no, but chasing? Yes. He kept quiet and allowed her to continue. What was the point in arguing?

     "The cloth is the void, the nether. It has many names, and it is where Lilith was trapped. It is the place where nightmares are born and raised, a place where the worse things imaginable exist. When Lilith escaped from there, she tore a hole in a fabric of reality. She broke the rule that should never have been broken. The rip got more extensive over time, and more things escaped. She jumped from world to world, causing more cracks, letting more seep through.
Letting things escape. Others, well, some wanted to get in".

     "Why?" Daniel asked.

"Why wouldn't they?" Crystal replied as if it was the most stupid question anyone could have ever asked. "You have the secrets of it all there. This is a place where nobody was ever meant to step foot. I do not know if God is real, but I am pretty sure the Devil is. Imagine, though, if God was real? If he had this area where he kept his secrets. To peek behind the great wizard's curtain to see something that was meant to be hidden forever, Gods sandbox". The enthusiasm dripped from her voice as she spoke. Her eyes lit with a burning fire of passion, "Imagine being able to see it all from the outside and to understand things. To be able to answer the question, why?"

"All while being eaten by a giant squid monster that can only be imagined and is the evilest thing ever created", Lisa added.

"Oh", Martin said, a trifle disappointed. The idea of seeing it all and understanding it was enticing, and who wouldn't want to see that? "I don't think we could even if we wanted to", Crystal said. "I think only the dead can walk those plains. I suspect there are rules in place to stop us, mortals, from entering".

"So then, what is the point in telling us this?" Daniel asked. "If we can't get there, then how is it relevant".

"There are places in the world, our world, but no doubt others too", Crystal continued, ignoring Daniel, "Places where the veil is weakened, where it is relaxed or broken. Torn by Lilith's actions. I think the house sits on one of those places. I think the house was a gateway designed to stop things from getting out, and I think whoever owned that house before tried to use it to get in".

"Faustus!" Daniel said without thinking. He moaned the name under his breath. "Was that his name?" Crystal asked without much interest. "Well, I suppose he is the one behind this. I think he entered the nether, and then when you burnt the house down, he escaped".

"It can't be", Lisa said, "I remember all of that from the time. Daniel saw Faustus in the house and grounds".

Crystal shook her head as she thought. "I don't know", she said, finally. "Maybe being that close to the tear, to the schism between it all means that echoes can escape? Maybe what you saw were ghosts?"

"Maybe you're all mad..." David said out loud. he liked them, he couldn't have told you why, but he found himself feeling at home with them. "Maybe..." Crystal said dejectedly. It made David feel a little guilty for saying it out loud. "Sorry", David said, "I am just struggling with this".

"No, no. It is fine", Daniel said. "I am usually the cynical one. It always helps to have a cynical voice".

"But still, you don't believe all this do you?" David asked. Daniel sat for a moment before he replied. Throwing ideas around his head before speaking. "I know what I saw when I went to that house", he said. "I know the housekeeper in the kitchen was there. I know that the well in the basement was". He stopped for a moment. Searching for the word. "Haunting? Disturbing? Oh, I don't know", he said. "Look, it scared the shit out of me. It was unnatural. Then when I got outside, I know Faustus was there. Finally, I know that I shot myself and that I died".

"You did what!" Crystal shouted and causing Lisa to jump. "You died
on the site of that house, and you only bring it up now?"

"They knew", Daniel said as he pointed his finger at Lisa and Martin. "Besides, the quack said it must have been shock or something. He said there is no way that I died with a gunshot to the head".

"You were shot in the head?" David asked.

"Yes..." Daniel started and then stopped. "No, I don't know. This is all I have left". Daniel tapped the scar on his forehead. "I shot myself, and somehow I survived". Crystal looked at him with the look of someone who had just bought a vegan burger, only to find out it was real meat. "Suicide? Suicide, in a place where the tears are thinnest? Oh goody, I am so glad you told me this as soon as we met" Crystal stood up and turned to leave. "Don't come near me; stay away from me. I want nothing to do with you", she said whilst looking specifically at Daniel and then stormed from the room. "I'll go after her", Lisa said as she stood. She left more mildly than Crystal. "She is braver than me!" Martin said with a smile, trying to lighten the mood.

"What about you?" Daniel asked David, "What are you going to do?"

"My mother always told me not to rush into things", David said. "I have a lack of imagination, and at times I can't think outside the box. It makes me a decent enough copper because most things play out as you'd expect. If you suspect the employee who is missing has stolen the money, then they probably have".

"And if they haven't?" Daniel asked. David looked at him. He had a look of sadness and loss on his face. "Then you dig, and you keep searching until you find something that fits. I can't sit there and say, what if this or what if that. I need facts".

"So you don't believe this?" Martin asked. David held his hands out once more, palms upwards, as he looked at Martin. This is what I am, his gesture said. "Guys, I'm a pragmatist. I need something I can hold, something I can squeeze. I can't take this back to my boss. She'll think I've finally flipped and have me pensioned off. I do know that I saw nobody escape from that car. I was watching the whole time. Unless I blanked, and I do not think I did, nobody walked away. So I am searching the pieces for answers, trying to fit it all together".

"So?" Martin asked.

"I told you. I am going to dig. I am going to dig into that house and see what I can find".

They dug. The three all dug and looked for anything that could help. David did what he did best, and he looked into the history of the house and grounds. He found it difficult to believe what they did, but he couldn't explain everything logically. That bothered him. If he could not explain it using logic, then what if they were right? The car had been empty - *apart from the mannequin* - he was sure of that.

The child and his parents. No drugs and no signs of any previous abuse, self-inflicted or otherwise. They had, so it seemed, fucked and ate each other. David sighed. He was still ignoring the facts. They had fucked and eaten each other. The doll had been used to attack the child; was it possible, he thought, could it be? Doll and mannequin, he let the idea turn on his mind. They were similar, but was being similar enough? It would not have been enough in any typical case, but was this a routine case? What if the things Crystal had said were true?

Then he had the Church, another bizarre one. Some parishioners had traces of minor drug use, but nothing major. A little pot and other minor things. Just a smattering of insignificant drug use here and there, but nothing that could explain what happened. David had wondered if it was a Jim Jones type of affair. The American Cult Leader had taken his flock to Guyana and then killed so many of them in a *mass suicide*. It was, as with the family before, all bizarre and unexplainable. The sexual aspect was also a link between the family and the church.

The thief, now this one did have something, maybe nothing, but it was something.

The case file for the car that he had stopped had come through that morning, and it was a mess. Signed everywhere to make sure everyone knew it was *a preliminary report* and filled with lots of facts but so few helpful clues. The car had been stolen and reported as such. The lady who had witnessed the theft had been a victim. *Coincidence?* All the witnesses had seen the mannequin, and none had seen anyone else in the car. A few had been - *understandably* - hesitant about reporting a car being driven by a store mannequin. Still, when explicitly asked, they had confirmed it. This was all good stuff, and it confirmed what he knew but was loathed to admit to himself. The mannequin was driving the car. He had almost thought *it appeared to have been driving*. He was falling into the same trap again. Failing to follow the facts, no matter how strange they seemed. The facts said that nobody had seen anyone but the mannequin.

There was a link, a connection between the two events. It could be nothing, but it could be something. When you have nothing, then you grasp at anything, he smiled to himself. It was a thing that many of his younger colleagues may not have noticed, but the way the car had been hotwired was intriguing. People leave clues everywhere, and they scatter evidence as if it were confetti at a wedding. Very few people can cover themselves when it comes to their style. It is an artistic fingerprint of criminality. Thieves will use the same method of entry year after year. An arsonist will repeatedly set the same fire type, and a car thief used the same techniques every time. An imprint of style. Newer cars filled with all the technology and computer gadgetry confused him. Had the car been newer, he'd have never seen the connection. Luckily the car had been older, and because of that, the link was as plain as day.

David still referred to it as an old-school method; it was in these days really rather ancient. The thief had used too many wires. They had only needed to use four in this car but had opted for five. That was not all. The twisting of the grounds had been done in a double twist and fold. Suitable for reliability but quite unusual in this day and age. Was it a coincidence? Was it just one of those things? He looked at the report of the thief that lay on his desk. Five wires, double twist and a fold... But this guy's head had been smashed in, so he couldn't have stolen the car, could he? But then, with this case…

Crystal soaked in her bath. She had needed to wash the anger from herself. To cleanse herself of the annoyance that she felt. She was angry at herself for losing her temper, she was angry at Daniel, but mostly she was angry that she would have to put this right. The other reason she was bathing was that she always thought better when lying in hot bubbly water. Lisa sat in the front room with a glass of wine. Crystal put her head back and tried to relax; she couldn't. She would close her eyes and try to touch the house and grounds, just a light, tender tickle of a touch. She could reach so far and then came unstuck, like trying to grab the last crisp from a tube of Pringles, only she couldn't turn the house upside down and shake it free. Every time her spectral fingers could feel the rough edges, she was pushed back by something. Once again, she almost had it when her hand was pulled from the spiritual tube.

Lisa sat and sipped the wine. Not bad, not bad, she thought absently to herself. She had a problem to solve, and the problem was this, how to get Crystal to help them. She felt that they needed her. Daniel may have supposed different, but she could, *and would*, handle him. Martin would do as he was told, and that just left the Policeman, David. "I can do nothing about the Policeman", Lisa said quietly to herself, "So push it from your mind, he will see that we were right in the end". Crystal though... What to do about Crystal.

"So, what do you think?" Martin asked Daniel.

"I think we're fucked", Daniel replied.

"Could be, could be", Martin said while he reached down into the drawer of his desk. Martin's hand re-emerged with a bottle of rum; he then went back and grabbed two glasses. "Want one?" He asked Daniel.

"No thanks, I am giving it a miss. Still recovering from this morning", Daniel said as he shook his head. "What do we have on both Faustus and the house?" Daniel asked. He shoved a load of paperwork to one side so he could use Lisa's desk. "It's not much", Martin said as he handed the files over. "But it is all we've got".

Lisa was sat with her back to the door when it slammed open, and as such, she nearly jumped from the chair. "I know what I need to do", Crystal said as she came into the room. She walked across the room, poured herself a glass of wine and sat opposite Lisa. Crystal leaned forwards and picked up her drink with a long towel wrapped around her and her hair wet and sticking to her shoulders. "So you're in?" Lisa asked. Crystal sighed, breathing out heavily through both nostrils before replying. "I don't think I have a choice. This thing is coming no matter what I do". Lisa had been worried about how she was going to convince Crystal. She looked over at the other woman and saw a determination. Now she worried about what Crystal had planned.

# The Ex-Boss

TO: Joanne.Rivers@BWPD-internal

FROM: David.watson@BPD-internal

SUBJECT: Advice

Boss / Ex-Boss. I need some help. I have something quite bizarre in a case, and

I don't know where else to turn. I know you have a little experience with this, so I am hoping for some guidance. If you have the time…

-------------------------------------------------------------------------

TO: David.watson@BPD-internal

FROM: Joanne.Rivers@BWPD-internal

SUBJECT: RE-Advice

Hit me, David. What is up? I will help where I can. --------------------
---------------------------------------------------------

TO: Joanne.Rivers@BWPD-internal

FROM: David.watson@BPD-internal

SUBJECT: RE-Advice

Okay. I shall start where I think all this started.

We have a haunted house (alledged!) that caused an investigator to go into shock (CF BPD4X8746Q)

Next, the same investigator burns said house to the ground. (CF BFD5G7463R)

Nothing too strange thus far; this is where I get lost, so stay with me.

CF - BPD8D3755W - Death of Thomas Hopkins. Known car thief.
CF - BPD8E3798W - Death of Greg, Molly, and Grant Chapman

These cases happened in Marshfield lane, and I have a hunch (between ourselves) that they are connected.

CF - BPD1E7495E - Fire and deaths at Our Lady and the English Martyrs Church.
CF - BPD6Y3820D - Theft, hit and run, and pursuit of a vehicle.

This one I can comment on as I was the pursuit vehicle. I picked up the chase and pursued the vehicle. The chase continued down Seaview road and onto the seafront. I cut through the town centre, hoping to intercept.

I managed to cut up through Pier Street and catch them just before the Southern

Esplanade. I managed to disable the chase car. That was… DRIVERLESS! I know logically it can't be driverless, but I did not see anyone leave the car! There was nobody at the scene who looked like they may have slipped out. Just a mannequin, an old school shop mannequin. It is crazy. Logically it can't be what I saw, but I promise you it was!

Then, and this is where I really can't join the dots. The Institute for Paranormal affairs was the car being chased, and they seem to think all the cases are linked!

I really do not know where to go with this. I know you like this strange stuff so I would value your opinion. Off the record, of course.

David.

---

TO: David.watson@BPD-internal

FROM: Joanne.Rivers@BWPD-internal
SUBJECT: RE-Advice

**Off the record.**

I'd actually already read the first case files, and I have just read up on the chase. My first words of advice would be to trust The IPA. They are good at what they do, I may not always agree, but they know their shit.

Secondly, I will back you. If you need something, then please, Let me know.

Thirdly, and finally. Try emailing seanroberts@srpi.co.uk. Yes, I know it's a PI, but trust me on this. Let him know I sent you. He can help!

Keep the SECOND point in mind. I will be pissed if I find out you did not ask for help when it was needed.

Joanne.

---------------------------------------------------------------------------

TO: seanroberts@srpi.co.uk

FROM:
david.watson9567@gmail.com

Subject: Advice - Joanne Rivers.

Hi.

Joanne has recommended that I contact you about some cases I am working on. Several aspects seem confusing to me, but I think they may be linked, and she said you could help.

Is there any chance I could pop over and have a chat?

David.

---

TO: david.watson9567@gmail.com
FROM: seanroberts@srpi.co.uk
SUBJECT: RE- Advice - Joanne Rivers

David.

I am busy until the weekend. I can see you anytime then, so pop over on Sat?

Sean

---

TO: seanroberts@srpi.co.uk
FROM: david.watson9567@gmail.com
SUBJECT: RE- Advice - Joanne Rivers

Saturday is good. I will pop over in the morning, say 10am?

David.

---

TO: david.watson9567@gmail.com
FROM: seanroberts@srpi.co.uk
SUBJECT: RE- Advice - Joanne Rivers

David.

Sounds good. For now, trust the IPA and work with Joanne where you can (yes, she contacted me and gave me a quick briefing).

Egress could be something. It could be nothing. Be cautious and take the help!

Sean.

# The Decision

They had all agreed to meet back up at the Institute to discuss what they had found and what they would do next. Lisa, Martin and Crystal were all there when David and Daniel had finally arrived. David sat down in a chair. The chair wheezed as he did so, letting out a breath of dead air. He was then the first to talk. "Here is what I am going to do", he said. "I am going to listen to what you have to say. I will comment only when I need something to be clarified or if I can add information in some way. *I am trying guys*, I will try to not be cynical and to help where I can". Lisa handed David a cup of coffee, "That's fair enough. That is all we would ever ask", she said as she did so. Lisa turned to Martin, "Tell us what you know", she instructed.

"There is not as much as I would have liked", Martin said. He opened a file that he had on the desk and started to speak. "Everything about the house, Egress, was quiet until the eighties. We are not dealing with some Amityville style house here with multiple events, not at that point anyway".

"Amityville was nonsense", David added. Martin looked at him with an uncomfortable smile, "I know. I was keeping it as layman as possible", he said before continuing. "Then Faustus

McGovern buys the house, and we know all about Faustus". Lisa took over as if on cue.

"Faustus was thought to be a crank throughout much of his life. It was mostly before our time, obviously, but we have the files and the reports. He started out in the sixties and seventies. He came to our attention then, and in the eighties, we got involved. He would be peddling his fortune-telling and spiritualism. There is no evidence that he was anything other than a sham, a charlatan. He would play one town and then move on to the next when the place got too hot. Something changed though, in the nineties".

Lisa took a sip from her cup and looked to make sure everyone was listening. "Then he started to get more interested in anything and everything supernatural or otherworldly. We have multiple statements and reports that his bookshelves began to grow. He had never shown too much interest before, but now he was becoming quite the bibliophile. First, he had the fiction, the Wheatly, Lovecraft, etcetera. His taste then started to focus on the darker and more forgotten works. He dropped from the radar then, confining himself to the house. Many thought he had become a recluse, a lock-in. It was presumed he would die old with the house and be found one day, alone and dead".

"We could never work out what he was doing", Martin said. "We knew it must be something. You don't just change. But, we could not make anything stick".

### **The Past**

"Faustus, are you sure?" Meredith asked him tepidly. Faustus turned and looked at her. His black hood hung over his shoulders, "Do you doubt me, woman?" he asked, not kindly but without raising his voice. "No, no. You know I don't", Meredith replied and sulked away timidly. Faustus ran his fingers over the pages in the old book for one last time. The ripples in the old paper are almost like a fingerprint of its own. He read the words in his own head, just as he had read them a thousand times before. He could feel it, taste it in the air. Tonight was the night he would meet his idol; tonight, he would learn all he had ever wanted to know. He lifted his hood over his head and stood up. He took the book from the table, held it under his arm and made his way down to the basement.

He took the steps one be one on his way down, careful not to trip or fall. The girl lay tied and bound just as he had left her. Faustus walked to her and checked the knotting, pulling it hard as her screams muffled the gag. "Calm yourself my dear", Faustus said. She had been wandering the streets when they had found her, a vagabond, a wastrel, nothing more important than a rat. "You should be grateful to us", he said as he sat upon the edge of the well. She had been nothing, and now she was going to be part of something, something magnificent.

"You should be happy. You are now more important than you have ever been", he said, toying with her. Unsurprisingly, the truth was that he did not give a shite what she thought or what she felt. She was just a useful object to him, just a walking and talking piece of meat, and he liked to play with his food. "I am going to give you some strength to help you with what is to come", Faustus said. "It won't take all the pain, but it will take enough". Faustus used the middle finger on his left hand, pushing the nail into his right palm. He dug deep until the skin broke and then dragged the nail along. He squeezed his hand into a fist and let the blood drip onto the rag in her mouth. Faustus watched as some of the blood crept in at the corners. The blood making its way into her mouth, his and her lives connected. "Now sleep", Faustus said, and as if she were hypnotised, she did just that.

There were just the three of them in the basement, Faustus, Meredith and the woman tied and lying on the floor. A six-foot stake had been forced into the ground. Smaller bits of wood had been piled in a triangular shape around its base. Faustus turned to look at Meredith and said, "Put her on it". She did as she was told. Not an utterance of doubt escaped from her. The woman was still asleep, still under the spell that had been weaved. Meredith grabbed her by the hair and pulled her toward the stake. She woke instantly and tried to scream, only for the screams to be muffled by the gag in her mouth.

*The vision Daniel had seen had been different? Was it fake? A Chinese whisper of a dream?*

The woman tried to fight back, but with her arms and feet tied tightly, she could do nothing as Meredith dragged her along the earthy floor. She is just a short, slim woman, and this woman dragged her with ease. Meredith pulled her up and stood her next to the stake. The woman played dead for a moment, trying to shake all her weight. A deadweight being harder to manage. Meredith just grabbed her by the neck and pushed her head against the post. The woman smelt the sweat on Meredith's' hand as she pushed her neck backwards. Meredith raised her other hand; it was fisted. When it was right in front of the woman's face, she lifted the index finger and waggled it from left to right. She shook her head as she did so. Quick as a flash, she had another piece of rope and had wrapped it around her neck, removing her hand briefly to do so. Meredith made her way behind the woman, holding the rope at her neck tight, and tied it. She had no choice now. If she flopped again, the rope would likely strangle her where she stood. Meredith wrapped one final rope around her waist and tied it tight. She was bound and unable to do anything. Meredith's pupils whirled with enthusiasm for the task that she would now undertake. She had a small bottle and in that container was a black liquid. She poured it all over the wood at the woman's feet. She then lit it with a match, and the smokeless flames started to grow.

The flames crawled at first, making their way up the wood that had been carefully laid for them. The warmth climbed to just below her feet. She dared not look down. The heat rose along with the flames until they tickled her feet.
She could feel the tightening of her skin as the flames took root. These unnatural flames climbed slow. She felt the pain and, *gag aside*, she wanted to scream out, but she could not. It was like her brain had compartmentalised it, pushed it away to the back of the cupboard. Hidden from her, but still there, ready to emerge. Her skin hardened with the flames, and now it cracked. She felt every stretch, creak, and snap as it broke. The dress they had put her in caught aflame; the fire had taken hold now. Her skin popped as it burnt like the crackling of bamboo on a campfire. The pain niggled and nagged like a dull throbbing headache. It was just on the edge of tolerance for her, and she would have broken screaming into the gag had it got worse. Still, she begged for this to be over. The dress was fully aflame, her skin acting as a reverse candle, the fat and muscle acting as a wax substitute for the outside wick. The fire leapt from dress to shoulder and then to her hair. The familiar smell that she had smelt many times now engulfed her nostrils. The hairspray she had used on her hair cheered the flames on until her whole head was

immersed in fire. The fluid in her eyes boiled, and then darkness took hold.

Suddenly the ropes gave, and she fell forward to the ground. The ropes, her dress, and the gag all burnt away to dust in the unnatural smokeless flames. It hurt, and that is what she remembered. It was stupid really, *oh hi darling, yes I was burnt at the stake, but do you know what really hurt? It was hitting the ground afterwards.* The burnt husk of her remains convulsed on the floor. Writhing like the pictures in a flipbook that were slightly out of sync. The things that were once her ears. The hardness that had burnt to a crackling heard the voice that said, "Get the girl". She felt her arm being grabbed, the skin flaking away, and then she was pulled. Skin pulling from bone, bone slipping from muscle as she was dragged. She let out a groan as she is hauled. A groan that escaped from a mouth that is now as dry as an old tobacco pouch. Nobody heard it, or if they had, they did not acknowledge it.

She was lifted into the air, and she can feel the coolness on the crisp remains of her skin. Just as quickly as she had been lifted, she was then dropped, and she was falling. Falling, but falling too far. Plummeting somewhere that is lower than the ground. Oh God, the well, she thought. God has a sense of humour, *maybe*? Her leg hits the wall of the well as she falls. She can imagine the voice. *Hey girl, you got it; it's the well.* The knee hit next, with the burnt skin and muscle being stripped from it like heated paint falling and peeling from a wooden beam. The leg snapped at the knee, but it somehow still held together. Her flame-grilled body still doing enough to hold on even as she bounced to the other side. Her shoulder took the brunt of the force this time. She tried to grab a hold of the walls to slow her fall. Her fingers just snapped, the skin peeled from them as she tried to grab anything. Then she hit the bottom of the well, a long, deep, dried hole in the ground. So thank you, Lord, she thought, it was all over. Only it wasn't; she was still alive. Then the well shaft heated. It got hotter and hotter as she lay there. Her skin started to fall from the bone and melt into the stone she lay upon. What was left was being burnt away by the heat. Muscle flaked and burnt in the flameless heat until all that was left was bone.

The two of them circled the well. Faustus held his book aloft. "And let there be light", he shouted. "But, with the light comes a darkness, the mother of darkness".

"Mother of darkness", they both chanted together. Faustus pushed the book forwards, holding it over the centre of the well. The book burst into a blue flame, and Faustus held it steady. The blue flame danced up and down his arm but did not leave any damage or burn him. "Let there be light", he said once more as he dropped the book. The book fell six inches and then hovered above the well. The blue flame moved above it and then shot out in two directions.

Meredith and Faustus screamed as the piercing blue blaze ripped through them. Their arms raised, and for just a moment, they looked like the dancing wind puppets you see outside some businesses. The flame spikes retreated back into the book, and for a second, everything was still. The book hovered, and the two believers stood, then they dropped. Bodies and book hit the ground at the same time. The book fell down the shaft, the bodies to the soiled ground. *Oh, you do like your fun and games*, Faustus thought as he lay on the floor and looked around the room. He could see his companion; she was dead. She had died the instant the blue streak had hit her. Why was he left alive? He tried to move but found he couldn't. He could move nothing other than his eyes. His body was paralysed from the tips of his hair to his big pointed toenail. He lay on the floor, and in his head, he screamed.

### Back to the Now

Lisa talked and had been talking for a while. "Only Faustus's body was ever found".

"So just him and Meredith?" David asked. "I saw nothing in the reports about anyone other than Faustus". David looked down through some of the paperwork that he had. "We can't be sure, of course", Martin said. "I did the research on this one, and the closest I could find was an old summoning ritual. Two believers, a well and a book, are needed along with a sacrifice. We never found Meredith nor the sacrifice. It was not through want of trying, I can tell you! The well was never an original feature. It had been added afterwards. That was how I managed to find the correct ritual they were using. What I think is the correct one. I thought they were drawn to the house because of the well, but maybe it is as Crystal said, and it was because of this tear".

"It is", Crystal said adamantly.

"Maybe, Hell - pardon the pun – probably", Martin said. "What is important is that we never found two critical things. A good ritual needs a book, and this one did. It also needed a sacrifice. We could find neither". Martin took a breather for a moment, letting Lisa continue. "So, we sent someone down the well. They found nothing. They said there was a small tunnel, but as a sacrifice is what it is, we saw no point in further exploring. Costs and the tunnel size made it exorbitant".

"I think that was a mistake". Daniel said. "I saw something burrowing up
from the floor. I think there is something, someone down there".

"After all this time?" Martin asked.

"Have you ever considered that the sacrifice might be the solution to this?" Crystal interrupted. "Like in old ghost stories, how the spirits cannot pass on until they are all laid to rest? In this one, you still have an undiscovered body, lay that to rest, and it may". She stopped for a moment. "I am stressing the word *may*. It may move Faustus on. He is out of the void, he is in our world, and he has to play by our rules".

"It feels like a long shot, a shot in the dark", Daniel said.

"Do you have anything better?" Crystal quickly replied.

David sat and watched them, taking this all in, and finally, he spoke. "I can tell you a few things you have missed. The first is something you could not possibly have known. That is, unless you had someone leak police files, and if you did, I'd want to know who. Faustus did not die straight away".

"What?" Daniel asked, shocked.

"He did not die for some time. Faustus died of starvation and dehydration, and It took a while".

"You didn't think that odd?" Lisa asked.

"Sure, but we are policemen. No one was reported missing. There was no sign of foul play. We went down the well and found nothing of interest. It was all weird, it all made little sense, but you can only go where the evidence leads. In this case, the evidence led nowhere. Technically the case is still open. A few officers took an interest when you burnt down the house". David nodded in Daniel's direction. "The second thing I am surprised you missed", David said. This time he smiled, "Have you ever looked at the house from above?" One by one, they shook their heads. "Well", David said and held out a photograph. They each looked at it with a blank expression on their faces. "If you look. You have the road and then one that intersects it. The intersecting roads are both cul-de-sacs. It is not too much of a stretch to see". David handed them a second photo, this time with a red marker drawn on it. He had drawn a line straight down the main road and up the house's driveway stopping at the front door. He had then drawn another line along the intersecting road that began and ended in a cul-de-sac. It was a crucifix. "The well would be like the dot above the letter 'i'", he said.

"How did we miss this?" Lisa asked, angry at herself more than anything.

"I want to get a look in that well", Daniel said.

"That might be tricky", Martin added. "There are remains of a burnt
house above it".

"How much will it cost to clear?" Daniel said. Lisa just looked resigned and loaded up the Institutes accounts program.

None of them noticed the translucent cloud hazily hovering just below the window, *and why should they have*? Would you? It could not hear what they were saying. It was wary of this group. Something deep within warned it that they were a danger. It needed to know why. What danger could they possibly pose? These tiny insignificant ants. It had seen the void, and it had seen what lay beyond this world. It had spoken to the Goddess of Darkness herself, so why? Why did it feel afraid?

David was outside having a cigarette when Daniel left the office. Had he been waiting for me? Daniel thought. As if to answer the question, David wandered over, "Just the man I was waiting for", he said. "I did some digging, and I think it is for your ears only. I don't think it relates too much to what you're dealing with". Daniel looked at the Policeman, not really interested in all truth. "What is it?" he asked politely. David read people well, and he could see that Daniel had other things on his mind, so he got straight to the point. "The house was sold shortly after that", Daniels interested peaked. "It was sold to a man via a private auction. Nothing ever really became public, and it was all kept very hush-hush". David extended the 'sh' on the final 'hush'. "You'd be surprised at what a little pushing and a police identification can do".

Daniel thought that he would not have been at all surprised. Still, he let David continue. "Stephen Johnson bought the house". The cloud rippled above at the mention of the name. Had they been looking upwards, they would have seen a glimmer like oil floating atop of water. It did not last long, but it was a reaction nonetheless. "My Father", Daniel said. "Yes", he added in a dejected manner. "I never knew him", he added.

*Johnson, Johnson*! The cloud thought. It had learnt enough, and it dived at the two men. If this man was the son of Johnson, then it would take him here and now. It flew down, but then it stopped. *Not through choice*, it had still wanted to attack and consume them. It was held back from doing so by an unseen force. It was like an invisible boundary that had been placed around the men. It tried again and just smashed into nothing. Smashing back like a ball hitting a sheet of clear plastic. A female voice rattled through it, commanding it to stop. "He bought the house though and left it to you", David said. The two men were completely unaware of the cloud that had tried to infect them. "Why do you think he did that?" David asked. Daniel said that he did not know. He really thought that he did know. There was a feeling in his gut that had been rolling around down there for a few days. A jumbled mess of ideas about everything else, but this one felt right. This one gave him that feeling he got when he looked at a word and instantly told his mind that it was spelt correctly.

"He wants me to end it", Daniel said.

# The Help

TO: JoanneRivershme@gmail.com
FROM: seanroberts@srpi.co.uk
SUBJECT: Your friend.

Joanne.

Your colleague emailed me for help today, as you had said he would. I don't want to tell you how to do your job, but as you forwarded him to me, can I just say this. Look after him. I do not think this is anything, but it may be. I have certainly not heard anything. I have arranged to meet him at the weekend. I will be sorting something at Vegas until then, so it is the earliest I could manage.

Look after him Joanne, this may not be something a layman should be getting involved with.

Sean.

--------------------------------------------------------------------------

TO: seanroberts@srpi.co.uk

FROM joannerivershme@gmail.com
SUBJECT: RE- Your friend.

S.

I am literally about to email him. I am sending this, and then I am replying to a message he sent me. Nothing too serious at Vegas, I hope? Let me know if I can help.

J.

-------------------------------------------------------------------------

TO: David.watson@BPD-internal
FROM: Joanne.Rivers@BWPD-internal
SUBJECT: RE- Investigation

David, please trust me on this. I will get you what you need. I can't send backup, I wish I could, but this needs to be kept as low profile as possible. If it is nothing - as I suspect it is - then it'll be my arse on the line. I know you take risks at times, but I can't afford to be suspended. Spots, tape, and a hold on police action (to a point) are all arranged.

Protect them, David. I leave it in your capable hands.

Spoke to Sean, he said he will see you at the weekend.

Joanne.

---

TO: Joanne.Rivers@BWPD-internal
FROM: David.watson@BPD-internal
SUBJECT: RE- Investigation

Thanks for all the help, Joanne, and thanks for reminding me I am getting closer to retirement! I will make sure it all goes well. What do I have to lose anyway? Ha! Roll on tomorrow evening; I could use something interesting in my life right now.

David.

# Before the Storm

Daniel stood and watched as the bulldozers cleared the rest of the house. They pushed it away to one side like a child *tiding* their toys. The woods, metals, and plastics that had once been so grand, now creaked and groaned as they were pushed aside. Daniel needn't have been there, but something pulled him back to the site. A magnetic curiosity pulled him there. He hated not knowing. He finally had what he had always wanted, proof, but now he had to stop it. The problem was that he had no idea how to do that. He had no idea at all if what they were planning would work. The logic was well known, but what if the house fought back? He had seen what it could do.

The dust of long-dead things, skin, dirt, and others discarded crap floated through the breeze and settled in the early morning dew. The remnants of decades now reintegrating with nature. The trees had been cut back so the bulldozers could get to the site. The lane that led from the road now looked eerily like Daniel had seen on his first visit. He physically shook the feeling from his mind, now was not the time. "Keep the basement clear", one of the workers shouted to another as he spotted some of the house falling into what was the basement. "Yeah, yeah", his colleague shouted back as he repositioned so that no more debris would fall. He pushed the remaining pile over with the rest, and by lunchtime, they had cleared the grounds.

With the grounds cleared, the area that had once been the house was vast and empty. All that remained was the hole that had been the basement, and in that, another hole was the well. Daniel walked to the edge of the first hole and felt for any change in the temperature. It was still and calm. He felt nothing. No changes in the air, no noises, and no sudden warmth. He jumped as the pile of wreckage behind him wheezed. He spun on the spot and looked, waiting to see what would happen. Nothing happened, as it was just the wreckage settling into place. Finally, he released his breath and headed away from the grounds and the hole. He walked the lane and once at the end lifted the police tape that now cordoned the whole site and walked out below it.

Lisa placed her hand where the wing mirror had once been on her car and whispered to it. "I'll get you fixed", as she leant on the door. She had just finished on the phone with the workers that had been hired to clear the site. That had not been cheap, she sighed. Especially as they needed the work done straight away, it had taken some favours and extra payments. Still, they had it completed in the end. They had told her of the man at the site. She knew it was Daniel before they had described him. He was worrying her. Since he had burned the house, his actions were erratic and unlike his usual robotic self. She was concerned, but at the same time, her gut told her to trust Daniel. He was usually at his best when pushed into a corner. He was in so many ways like her father, and that was one of the reasons she had broken it off. She was always aware of how things would look. She always considered the fact some would see her as dating an employee. She did not have daddy issues. *Still*, anyone who knew her family history would see the similarities between Daniel and Alex. She let her fingers rest on the empty hole in the side of the door and let out a sigh. She did love him, and she hated to let him go.

Martin sat and spoke on the phone, "so the spots and gennys are sorted?" He tapped the desk as he closed the file he had been reading. "All sorted", the reply came from David. "And, you have cleared the site?" he asked.

"It was finished about ten minutes ago", Martin replied.

"Blimey, you guys work quick!" David said before asking, "Tell me something, why do we have to do this at night?"

"Lisa works quickly, I think before I leap. At night? Why do you think ghosts and other things are only seen at night?" Martin asked.

"It's dark", David replied in his cynical but now friendly fashion, "people get the willies and see things in the dark". Martin had expected a reply like this. He liked the Policeman and always liked having someone cynical on board. "Sure, but it is mostly just a few simple things", Martin said and then continued. "You have the darkness, everything evil that is human, and many things not, like the darkness. Then you have peace. It is usually quieter".

"So that is it?" David asked with his curiosity piqued.
"There are other thoughts on the subject, but they are just that thoughts. You have the idea that it is easier to commune with them at night and that they were created of darkness, so they are easier to find in darkness. But, that could just be mumbo-jumbo".

"Ha!" David laughed down the phone, "I like you guys, you shoot straight. I may not understand, but I like you".

Crystal sat back and closed her eyes. She was at home now, in her domain and safe for now. She felt things that the others did not. They - *except for the Policeman* - knew tonight would be eventful, but they had no idea of the danger. Only, that wasn't entirely true, she thought. They knew it would be dangerous as they had done this type of thing before, but they had no idea of the scale of the danger. If they usually dealt with level five hauntings, this was a level ten. How did she know this? She knew it because *she was scared*, and Crystal did not fear the dead. She had been living with her *gift* for so long now that she was not afraid of these things. This was something else, and she could sense that. It scared her, but at the same time, it excited her. Like a rock climber who has just discovered a new, higher, mountain she relished the idea of discovering something new.

      Crystal leant forwards and grabbed her cup of tea, black and strong it was just the way she liked it. She let the edge of the cup rest on her lip for a moment before taking a sip. She had several questions that she would usually like to have answered. Did Daniel Die? If he died, then how is he still here? Were they really trying to reach out to her? The mother of darkness? Crystal wanted the answers to these questions. She had to know. Was she real?

# The Eyewall of the Storm

The afternoon sun was setting when they arrived at the site. The place where the house Egress had once stood but was now nothing but a pile of rubbish. "Will they hold up if it rains?" Martin asked David and pointed at the generators.

"They will be fine", David replied with confidence. David walked to the generator and flipped the fuel switch. He engaged the choke and then pulled the cord. The generator fired on the first attempt, and the four massive spotlights that Joanne had arranged flooded the area with light. "Let there be light", Lisa said. Daniel walked to the pit that was once the basement and looked down into it. He still felt no change in the atmosphere from the well, and for that, he was grateful. "I think we should get started", Lisa said, concerned as she looked up into the sky. "It looks like rain is coming". Crystal skipped forward towards the basement, not slowing in her skip for one moment. "Well, come on then, let's go", she said with all the enthusiasm of a child wanting to visit a zoo. "You're bonkers", Martin said with a smile. "Maybe just a little", she replied with a laugh and continued her skip. David looked at them, trying to resist a smile. "I think you are all bloody nuts", he joked. "But, maybe nuts is what we need", he finished under his breath.

Daniel looked down into the pit and pushed the ladder that had been placed there with his foot. It did not move as he pushed it. "Sure it is safe?" he asked David.

"Pretty damn sure", David replied. He had to raise his voice a little as the wind started to pick up. Daniel stepped forward and descended the ladder. It was secured tight and did not move at all as he descended its struts. "I guess you were right", he called back up to David. Daniel continued to the well and found the equipment there ready for him. It was covered in a blue tarp; he ripped the tarp free and stacked some stones on it to stop it from blowing away. He pushed the spike that was in the ground with his foot. It was solid. He moved the one on the side of the stone circle that made the top of the well. He checked, and it too was stuck securely. "You don't have to do this", Lisa called down to him. The concern in her voice was evident to them all, even with the wind starting to howl a little. "One of us does. I am the best choice", Daniel replied, trying to keep all emotion out of it. "It is fine", he shouted to her, "I'd rather be down here than up there if this weather gets worse", he lied.

Daniel slipped the rope through the harness and carabiner before dropping the rope down the shaft. He felt for when it reached the bottom and had a good ten metres left. He let it fall freely until there was no more left. He stood on the edge of the well and lowered himself into position. He looked up at the clouds in the sky as he lowered himself. Maybe it wasn't a lie; the mist that seemed to be forming along with the clouding sky looked ominous. He let himself drop a little and descended into the darkness.

The spotlights being lit had drawn a crowd to the cordoned off grounds. They had gathered in the cool evening air, ignoring the rain and wind, instead choosing to gawk at what was happening in the once quiet neighbourhood.
"What's going on?" A woman asked.

"No idea love", another replied. Still, they gathered and watched. Unable to see anything but able to happily speculate as they stood just on the taped boundary. "Used to be haunted that house. Maybe it's an exorcism", someone piped up from the back.

"You need sage and Priests for that shit; besides, how do you exorcise a house?" Another answered.

Crystal called out to the three that remained. "Martin, that corner. Lisa, that one, David, can you take that one". She pointed as she spoke to the corners where she wanted them to stand. The three made their way to the edges and awaited further instructions. Crystal had taken on the voice and stature of a hard and stringent headmistress. She was going about her work professionally. The hippy flower power image and voice had been stored away to be returned to use at another time. "I need you to each close your eyes and just to focus on my voice", Crystal called out as she stood dead straight and upright with her skirt flapping in the wind. "I'm going to take us into the darkness to search for this girl", Crystal said. "If we find her, we may be able to end this! If we can find her name and body, we can send her on her way. I need you to all stay calm and listen to me". Her voice had taken on a rhythmic effect. It was almost like a ticking metronome speaking and delivering the words. Perfectly in sync and delivered with a precision she had spent many years mastering. "Focus on your breathing", she said in a metrically measured way. "Clear your mind as you breathe in, and then out", she said. "I want you to clear your mind and focus on your breathing. Then, in", she paused. "And out. In, and out. Imagine you are in the darkness. You are not worried, and you are not scared. You are just waiting.

Waiting for us to arrive".

Daniel could hear Crystal in his head. How she did it, he did not know, but he heard her soothing him as she spoke, encouraging him. "Just stick with it.
I am here with you. Here with you there and in the darkness here", she said. Daniel pushed his feet against the wall of the well and descended further. He looked down and could see the light reflected back at him from the stone base; he was about halfway. He looked

up, and he could see the moon in the small circle above. Darkness had fallen quickly.

The misty cloud split and headed in separate directions. Half headed for the rubble that had once been the house and the other for the crowd of people. The crowd did not notice the mist. They breathed it in willingly as they stood and gawked at the spotlights at the end of the long driveway. Once inside, they just stood staring, with no expression or emotion in their eyes or faces. Unblinking dead eyes gazed at the centre of the grounds. Their hands dropped beside them. The phones that many of them had held dropped to the floor and continued recording as they stood lifeless.

The rubble shifted, it was at first just a tiny minuscule movement, but two pieces seemed to join together. This was followed by a third and then a fourth. Like magnets with metal, piece by piece moved into place, joining the one next to it. The old child's toy that had used shards of metal and a magnet only now was plaster, wood, and other pieces of a house joining together. But, slowly. They crept together to avoid being spotted. It needn't have bothered.
Daniel was in the well shaft. The others were in the darkness.

Crystal stood alone in the dark, alone in the nothingness of space. The other three emerged, stepping forward from nothing to become something. Martin looked around and then said, "Where are we?"

"I call this the dreamscape", Crystal answered. "I have no idea what it is in technical terms".

"I've never heard of anything like this", Lisa said, awestruck. "How long have you been able to..." David interrupted her. He had a note of tension in his voice like a guitar string pulled tight and then snapped back. "I think we have a job to do. Can we leave the sightseeing and explanations until later?"

"We have to search for the girl", Crystal said. "She is here somewhere;
we have to find her".

"Can't you, I dunno, turn on the lights?" Martin said.

"You think she is the only thing here?" Crystal answered, "If we can't see them, then they can't see us". Martin gulped, and in the silent darkness, the other three heard it clearly.

Daniel was almost at the bottom. As he looked down, he could see the cold hard rocks that awaited him. Crystal was still in his head. How is she doing this, he thought. "You must tell us if you find anything", she said. "Anything at all, we need guidance". Yeah, sure. Daniel thought I'll just grab my mobile, although I doubt I'll get a signal. "No need", the voice of Crystal said in his head. Oh, that is very reassuring, he thought as his feet arrived and made contact with the cold, damp stone at the base of the shaft.

# The Eye of the Storm

From the centre of the rubble, something pushed its way through. What had once been wooden beams, wiring, and copper piping now pushed up through the middle. All joined together by the tangling of the clouded appendages. Sticking up in the air like a splint for a tree or a hand rising from a grave. It stood erect and still at six feet for a moment and then bent in the middle. The top half fell forward and lowered itself to the ground to create a triangle shape. The remains that it had emerged from twitched and shivered as it did so. The four that could have seen this happening paid no attention. They just stood staring into the hole that had once been the basement, captured in a hypnotic state as they traversed the darkness.

"He is at the bottom", Crystal said. Lisa opened her mouth and was about to ask how Crystal could know but then thought better of it. *Did it matter?* If she was right, she was right, if she was wrong? It made no difference to the task they faced. "Spread out, we have to find this girl", Crystal ordered. She took the voice of an officer this time, stern, strict, and direct, leaving no room for arguments. *Yes Ma'am*! David, Lisa, and Martin started to walk forward. Each of them holding their arms out before them and waving them slowly from side to side. They could see nothing in this darkness, so how could they expect to find anything? "Focus on the girl, try and imagine her in this place", Crystal shouted. Crystal closed her eyes and stepped forward. She had done this many times before, so she knew to trust her instinct. Were the others needed? Possibly not, but there is safety in numbers. When you are looking for the unknown, what harm could it do?

A second and third spike pushed through from the middle of the debris. Like the first, they extended into the air, then bent in the middle and placed themselves on the ground. A fourth, fifth, and finally sixth did the same. A strange triangular miniature, Stonehenge being formed from the ruins of the house. The mist, the fog, the cloud seemed to twist and twirl between the sections as it held them all together. The vapourless haze tangling together with the thing that once caged it. A rage had filled it, consumed it, and it gave it strength. The anger that could flow through a human with adrenaline was now proving it could drift through the smoky blur of cloud.

Daniel looked around. He shined the light from side to side and up and down. Daniel looked for anything that seemed important, anything that would give him some insight. He saw nothing. The hollow at the pit of the well was smaller than he would have imagined. It was barely six by six feet. He turned around and saw an opening, and he headed for it. The hollowed-out hole from years of water that had long dried up or been blocked elsewhere. Roots from trees and plants in the world above had bored through in places. They held together with the mud and stone protecting him, *he hoped*. Daniel scanned left and right as he made his way to the opening, the tunnel that had been mentioned. Shining his torch into the hole, he saw something white wrapped in a section of roots and grabbed it. It was a piece of paper. It should have long been long swallowed by the earth. Biodegraded and gone forever, but this piece was in pristine condition. He flipped it and looked at it for any writing, but it was blank. Just a blank, unblemished sheet of paper.

    Lisa threw her hands forward and grasped at nothing. She stepped forwards again into the nothingness of this dark space and tried to push the thought that this was pointless from her mind. Lisa thought of Daniel down at the bottom of the well's shaft. At least she knew where she was, *sort of*. She was not down a long, dark, and dank shaft. She thought about how she missed him. How she had broken it off, and the reasons for that. A twang in her chest snapped as she thought about this. She'd never been sure if it was the right thing to do. Sensible, logical even maybe, but right? Of that, she was not so sure.

With the jangly strum in her chest, she now knew it was the wrong thing. Sometimes you have to do the wrong thing for the right reasons. Lisa felt something, not physically but mentally. With the pain of regret and the thoughts of Daniel, she felt something in her mind fluttering and trying to escape. Blank and without any blemishes, she could feel it, could feel the friction of her fingers; it was a sheet of paper. She felt the friction in her mind as she pictured her fingers running along it. Lisa looked down at her hands and was shocked to find the page in her hand. The piece of paper that she had imagined was now a reality, and she was holding it. As authentic as anything in the darkness they were exploring. She looked at the page, and this time it had writing on it, she read it aloud. "Her name was Mary Watkins", Lisa said. Her voice seemed to come from the four corners of the darkness. The four of them all turned at once.

In the centre of them stood a woman, a girl.

Daniel shoved the page down deep into his pocket. He had no idea if it was important or not, but he kept it anyway. It felt important to him. He just sensed that he should keep a hold of it. The opening that he had found the page in was what held his interest. He approached it and saw that it was smaller than he had initially thought. There was a clawing around the hole, finger marks where dirt and mud had been dragged out. It only took a second to link the scratchings to the creature he had first encountered at the house. She had somehow, impossibly, tried to tunnel her way out. He looked into the tunnel, the light shining up, and could see the discoloured yellowing bone above. How had this been missed? Had it been here before? He could only see a little, but it was enough to confirm his suspicions. He heard a voice in his head; this time, it was not Crystal. It was Lisa. "Mary Watkins", she said aloud. The body, the remains, in the tunnel shivered slightly and then started to fall. Daniel stepped back to try and avoid them, and he tripped on a rock. Falling backwards onto his backside as the bones clattered to the ground beside him.

Lisa looked at the girl in the darkness and repeated her name, "Mary?" The four of them had now gathered together. Trying to find comfort in numbers as they stood in the darkness. They no longer needed to search as they had found what they were looking for. "You must go", Mary said and then giggled like a child. Her voice whispered and distant. It seemed to float towards them.
"It is not safe here".

"We came to help", Martin told her.

"I know", she said. "But you must go".

Crystal stepped forward. "How can we help?" She asked. Mary looked back at Crystal; a sadness filled her eyes. "You have to occupy it. You need to keep it busy". She giggled again, and this time it was a little unnerving. It seemed to come from the darkness itself.

"What?" Martin said, "How?" Mary looked at the sky, smiled at them and then spoke for the final time. "I want to speak to

Daniel. It is him I want to see", she said. Then clicked her fingers and vanished.

The four of them opened their eyes at the same time. They were stood in the same place and now were mildly damp. The rain had started to fall and sounded like drops of rice on a tin roof as it landed. They were stunned for a moment. Taking a second to get their bearings back, having been in Crystal's dreamscape. "What did she mean, keep it occupied?" Martin asked, then he heard the noise from behind. Martin turned and looked; the other's eyes followed his. The noise had come from the remains of the house.

# When the Levee Breaks

The rain started to hammer down, the tiny drops of rice that had been sounding on the tarpaulin had increased. It now sounded like the bag had split, and the rice was escaping at full speed. Pouring free at a thousand grains a second. Martin slipped on the wet ground, and David ran over. He managed to catch him just before he would have fallen into the basement. "You okay?" He asked as he helped him to his feet.

"Yeah, I'm fine. Where the hell did this come from?" Martin asked as the rain and wind continued to build. Both David and Martin looked for the two women and saw that they had their attention drawn elsewhere.

The six triangular struts lifted the centre, pulling more remains with them as it did so. It was slow at first but got steadier as it elevated itself. At twenty feet tall and thirty across, the thing was massive. "Jesus Christ", David said as he looked at it. His new curse words now becoming the most repeated thing in his life. The spider-like shape had risen, and it turned towards them. Its six legs lifted one by one, shyly at first, but it seemed to gain confidence as it turned. The strength it now felt inside was channelling through everything. This was more powerful than it could possibly have imagined. This mishmash spider-creature turned to face them. The furniture, plaster, wood, and everything else that had once made the house Egress combine as one with the cloud running through it all. "Run!" David shouted. David shouting snapped them out of watching, and they all ran. They ran as fast as they could back towards the entrance of the grounds. Lisa hesitated for a moment, "Daniel", she said.

> "He is at the bottom of the shaft. There is nothing we can do", Martin

said and grabbed her hand. Together they ran to catch up to Crystal and David.

Daniel sat with the bones around him, his backside wet from the floor. He no longer cared as the water soaked into his jeans. "So you were Mary", he said to the bones. "I am so sorry it took me so long".

"It was not your fault", a voice said behind him. Daniel jumped to his feet and spun around in one smooth action. It was something he would have never been able to do usually. The unease and apprehension flowed through him. She was standing moonlit in the centre of the shaft. "You did what you could, and I thank you", she said. Daniel looked at the girl. He felt nothing but sorrow for her. She had been put through Hell when alive and then stuck here after her death. How could she be so peaceful? How could she be so calm? So tranquil. As if reading his mind, she answered the unspoken questions. "I am free. After all these years, I am free", she said this as if it was the most crucial thing in the world to her. Like she did not know she would be sent on. That she could not stay here.

David, Lisa, Crystal, and Martin ran. They ran down the driveway towards the cross of the crucifix that made the roads. They could hear the spider-house moving toward them. The crunch and clattering as each leg eked forwards. It was slow at first, but they could hear it was gathering speed. They saw the crowd gathered and was starting to march in unison up the drive toward the house. The eyes on the members of the crowd dead as their feet moved in the zombie-like march. Not a goose step but more a zombie shuffle. "Jes..." David started, then stopped himself and corrected the curse to something else.
"Shit", he exclaimed, "We're going to have to fight".

David stormed forward and punched the first person he came to. It was a middle-aged man, and he went down without a fight. "Come on!" David roared back to the other three. Lisa marched on, Crystal and Martin followed behind.
Lisa pushed into the crowd, hitting some, slapping many and kicking others. David would have admired her gumption had he the time to look. David punched and kicked, Lisa kicked and punched. Martin pushed where he could, and Crystal hid behind Martin. She was a lover, not a fighter, as the song had said.

The house spiders wooden splinted feet crashed into the ground just behind them. It knocked the gawkers who were in the way to one side. One was unlucky enough to get caught under its foot. The wood and metal just splintered through the body like it was ice cream on a hot day. Blood rocketed out from the body and covered the house spiders leg. The body hung for a few seconds as the leg lifted once again. Finally, it fell into the mess of its haunted allies that had been either knocked aside or fell behind. Forever discarded and life cut short, it fell like a rag doll that had been emptied of its stuffing.

David pushed the crowd back and sideways so the others could get through, Lisa tried to do the same on the other side, but it was forlorn with her more petite frame. She could hold her own in most situations, but with these numbers, it was hopeless. "Run!" David screamed and pushed Martin and Crystal through. He stood, arms outstretched, trying to keep the zombified crowd from getting through. Lisa turned her head, "What about you?" she shouted.

"Just fucking run!" he yelled at her. She did not need telling twice. Lisa ran, Martin ran, and Crystal ran. They headed to Lisa's car that was parked at the crossroads.

David felt the horde behind him, the heat as they gathered and shuffled ever closer. He held his arms outstretched and expected the swarm to rush past him; they did not. Instead, they grabbed his arms and pulled them backwards. Yanking and pulling, he felt the tendons rip, then the muscle weakened, and finally, the skin tore. His arm was ripped and discarded, and the other followed straight after. Blood swam from him and into the crowd. He was pushed forwards to the floor, and the feet of the pack started stamping on him. He felt his ribs crumble as he was repeatedly kicked, stamped upon, and booted. When he saw the spider creature's foot heading towards his head, it was a blessed relief, and he welcomed it. His head was crushed under what was once a part of the hallway radiator, and David's tale had ended.

"All of this is a game to her", Mary said to Daniel. "That is what she
does. She plays games".

"Was what I saw real?" Daniel asked.

"Mostly".

"I don't understand", Daniel said.

"You are all just toys to her", Mary replied, as if that was an answer. She
held her hand to her mouth and suppressed a giggle. "I'll have nothing to do with her!" Daniel protested.

"She gave you life", Mary said. "She bought you back to play, and now you say that? How ungrateful you are". Daniel was unsure of what to say.
Unsure of what answer he should give.

Lisa pushed the accelerator to the ground, and the Cosworth engine thundered to life. The tires squealed as he slammed the car from first to second, and it roared down the road. The spider-house smashed through the gate at the end of the drive and gave chase. The gate fell apart like it was a pile of sticks, its metal bones splintering to the floor. "Faster", Martin screamed. Crystal kept quiet as she still remembered the look. "She told us to keep it occupied", Lisa spat back at Martin. The spider was hitting cars as it ran, knocking them aside.
The wooden legs breaking and then mending with the misty cloud that loomed over and between its parts.

"She bored of Faustus, so when you died, she bought you back. She thought it would be fun", Mary said. "She has protected you more than once now".

"Fun? Fun! People have died", Daniel shouted back. He stopped himself before he said more. "She cares not about that". Daniel felt a tinge, something drilled at his mind. A thought popped into his head. He did not know if it was right, but it was there, nonetheless. "Who are you?" He asked.

"I am Mary", she replied.

"I don't believe you", Daniel said, now feeling more sure of himself.

The spider-creature stopped suddenly. Lisa saw it in the rear-view mirror and slammed on the brakes. "It knows", Crystal said. "It knows something is wrong". The pieces of the house started to crumble and fall away as the mist drifted from it. Wood falling to the floor to be joined by the other shrapnel and debris. The cloud darted back towards the house, leaving the remains of what it had created to drop to the road. Lisa span the steering wheel and gave chase. The chased, becoming the chaser. Lisa closed her eyes as she smashed through the pile of rubble; the car screamed as it hit it. "I'm so sorry", Lisa said to the car. A piece of piping had got stuck in the front grill. It had cut a water pipe, and the car squealed as she tried to accelerate. The engine warmed and then overheated, and oil blew from the motor causing the bonnet to lift and painting it with a dark black steaming shine. The car slammed to a stop; the engine had seized. "We'll get it fixed sis", Martin said to Lisa as he opened the door and stepped out. The three of them ran back towards the house's grounds and saw the cloud escaping from the people who remained in the crowd. They all dropped to the floor, lifeless as it departed their bodies. It joined up with the other half and hovered momentarily. Still and waiting like it was considering its next move.

The girl smiled. "Would it make you feel any better if I said I was impressed?" she asked Daniel. "It usually takes longer, if they even get there at all". Daniel stood his ground. He had nowhere to go anyway. He asked once more, "Who are you?"

"Who do you think?" The girl asked.

"Lilith", Daniel replied. The girl stood for a moment and then clapped. A joyous clap that matched her smile. She giggled, clapped, smiled and bounced on the spot as if she had just been given the greatest gift of all time.

Everything stopped. Lisa, Martin and Crystal could still see everything, they could feel and hear everything, but they could not move. The cloud, too, just hovered like the unnatural thing that it was. Stopped like the jamming of an old projector reel. Raindrops continued to fall, and noises from all around continued to pass in waves. Everything else around the grounds of the house was still and quiet. "What the hell is going on?" Martin asked, relieved that he could talk.

"I have no idea", Crystal replied.

Daniel also found himself unable to move. He had no idea of what was going on with the others. He could only hope that they were okay. Crystal had long stopped replying to him in his head. "What have you done?" he asked.

"Given us time", came the reply. The girl morphed from an innocentlooking young lady into something else. Black boots with a black skirt with purple trim. A black shirt on top with hair draping over the shoulders. The hair was bleach blonde and tied on either side. The small space at the bottom of the shaft also changed. The stone walls seemed to expand like a rubber balloon being stretched. The six-foot hole became a twenty-foot room. The floor flattened, and large pillars of rock shrunk until everything was smooth. The walls opened up in places letting in a burst of impossible sunshine.

She looked at Daniel and leant against the wall beside her. "Do you like?" Lilith asked him.

"It's different", Daniel answered, unsure if she meant the room or herself. He tried to force himself to step forwards, but he couldn't; he was stuck like glue. "I used to think you can never have too much black, but now I think it's good to mix it up a little", she said conversationally as she twirled her fingers in her hair. Wrapping the hair around a finger and then letting it go, it sprang back into place. Daniel was in no mood for this. He worried about his friends. He worried about how he would escape, and he worried about the innocents that had been and would be harmed. "Is there a point to this?" He asked her. Lilith looked at the floor and pretended to sigh; it was a fake one, a child's loud one. She made as much noise as she could and then pretended to sob as she rubbed her eyes with lightly clenched fists. "It's called being polite, being conversational. Having a natter, a chin-wag. You get the idea; I am being nice". She stressed the final four words, her smile no more.

"Okay", Daniel said. He thought it better to be polite. To not poke the bear, as it were. "Okay then, down to business", Lilith said, smiling once more.
"You want Faustus to stop, correct?" She said.

*"No", Daniel said.*

Lilith stood stunned at this. She thought she had known what he would have wanted. "What do you mean no?" She asked with curiosity more than anger in her voice. The humour and good manners were gone, gone back to whence they had come. Daniel had to think, and he had to think quickly. He had a plan. He did not know if it would work. She liked to play games. That was what she had said. What had been written. He was about to take a gamble and play a game of his own. It was a high risk, high stakes, perhaps the highest. He rolled the die. "I want you to let Mary go", he said to her. She pushed away from the wall and stood for a moment, and considered. "Why?" She asked curiously.

"You've had your fun. She was innocent. Sacrificed in your name. Release her and take me instead". Daniel had not planned on saying the final part. Once he had started, it just oozed free. Running from him like a fully open tap. Pulling the Father Karras. "What if I say no?" Lilith asked. Daniel *had* expected this. He had already lined up the answer in his mind. "I think you will do what you want. You like to play. How can I stop you?" He asked and answered. Lilith stared at him. He could see intelligence in her eyes, a cleverness and deviousness. She rolled her tongue in her mouth, pushing it against her teeth. Then she opened her mouth and smiled once again. She continued to run the tongue over her teeth.

"Oh, that's clever", she finally said. Daniel's heart sank; he had gambled and lost. He had placed it all on black thirteen, and the ball had not even been close. "I free her, and then the tie that binds Faustus is gone. Is that the idea?" Lilith asked.

"Pretty much", Daniel admitted. *What was the point in lying*? If it were possible for his heart to sink to the very tip of his big toe, it would have done so.

It was over, and it was done. No extra life this time; he was staring at the game over screen with nothing left to play with. "Sure fuck it, why not!" Lilith said and flopped her arms down to her sides. Daniel's mouth dropped to where his heart had once been. He looked at her, unsure of if she was serious or not. Lilith lifted and then held her hand in the air, clicked her fingers and then vanished. Daniel suddenly fell forwards, much as the girl Mary had done when she had fallen from the stake. He was free, and he wanted out. Daniel blinked, and the room was gone. He was back in the hole at the bottom of the shaft. He ran back to the rope, wrapped it through the carabiner and started to climb.

The three of them stood, unable to move and saw it happen. They would have had trouble believing it had they not seen it. Even in the trade that they were in, this was a new one. A bolt of black lightning hit the cloud. It came not from above but from below, straight from the solid earth below. The cloud seemed to freeze and then shattered into a million pieces. It scattered the ground below it and then simply vanished. Absorbed into the ground, being sucked downwards perhaps to Hell. The rain and wind stopped just as suddenly, and the grounds were once again calm and quiet. They looked at each other with a bewildered look, unsure of what had just happened.

Lisa released first and ran straight for the basement. Martin and Crystal followed straight afterwards. Lisa lowered herself down the ladder, almost stumbling as she reached the bottom. Daniel was just popping from the well as she arrived. She grabbed him as he climbed over, hugging him and kissing him on the cheek. "What happened?" She asked.

"I think I made a deal with a deviless", Daniel replied. Daniel felt a warmth in his pocket, and he reached down inside. He pulled the paper from the pocket and looked at it. Lisa's eyes lit up. "That was the paper that told me the name of the girl!" She said excitedly.

"It was all a game to her", Daniel said as he unruffled the page. "She plays games. It was Lilith all along".

Daniel looked at the page, and now it had writing on it. It was a simple message, and he suspected it was meant just for him. He showed the others anyway.

*Thank you, Daniel, that was fun! We shall have to do it again sometime.*
*Toodle pip.*

It was signed with a single letter. "*L*".

# Epilogue

## *Faustus*

Faustus lay on the basement floor; it was only him left alive. Alive but unable to move, unable to do anything. *Why*? He thought. *We, I did everything right.* He was asking himself this question all the time, what had gone wrong? "Who says it didn't work?" A voice said. The voice was female, cocky, confident, and full of humour. "I do not suppose it ever occurred to you that I have no interest in being caged and controlled". Faustus tried to speak, he tried to move, but he was held in place by the darkness of black magic. His skin was falling from the bone from starvation. He was a meat bag with his bony skeleton poking through in places. Protruding through the skin as if all his bones had been neatly shrink-wrapped. He had forgotten how long it had been since he had eaten or drank anything. Days? Weeks? Longer? He had no idea.

"I am guessing you're hungry", she said. "I'd offer you some of my lunch, but you seem a little incapacitated". Faustus heard her lips smacking together as she licked a finger dry. Did she have something to eat? Did it matter? She was just toying with him. "I am sure by now you are starting to question the logic in summoning me. Maybe the idea that you should not have done it is rattling around in that skin suit, maybe it is not. I don't care". He had known it was her. Even before she had confirmed it, *he had known*. He had worshipped her, summoned her, and now she had him like this; why? "Oh my dear silly Faustus", she said. "Why? Why? Oh, Lilith, why do you do this to me!" Lilith laughed as she spoke, and she mocked him with her words. In many ways, that was more painful than the starvation and dehydration he had suffered to this point. "Why you do this to me Lilith?" When the one you love, the one you desire and worship mocks you and rebuffs you. That hurts more than any physical pain ever could. "I'll let you off a tinsy little bit because you are old fashioned, but I am not going to forgive you for everything. You would have used me for your own ends, and don't deny it. Oops, sorry, I forgot, you can't. Ha! It is quite a pickle you have gotten yourself into. Now, what are we going to do about this?" Lilith sat on the edge of the well. She swung her feet from side to side. At the same time, she said "Dum de dum" to herself out loud.

"Okay, yes, that is what we'll do", she said finally. "Any objections, raise your hands". She laughed loudly and wildly. "How silly of me", she said. "I keep forgetting that you can't. Oh silly me". Lilith pushed herself from the well using both and hopped to the floor. She walked over to Faustus and pushed his body over onto its back. Her heel sunk into his side. It pierced the flesh like a fork sticking into a raw sausage. She pulled her foot back and looked at him with disgust in her eyes. She wiped the heel as best she could on his robes. "Well, that was just gross", she said. Faustus begged for release from this. He begged to be free. "That is not very nice", she said. "You called me, and here I am. Now be grateful". Lilith pointed at the fire that had been set and then burnt. "I have no interest in that", she said, and the remains vanished. They melted away into the ground until all that was left was the soil. "I have no use for that daft fucker who was silly enough to follow you either", she grumbled as she turned her finger towards the corpse of Meredith. The ground opened up around the body, and it sank into it. Roots and vines gripped the body as it sank and tore at it. Tearing flesh from the bone and then the bone from muscle. Tearing them as quickly and efficiently as you would a sheet of paper.

The ground closed, and all the evidence left from the summoning was Faustus and Lilith. "Right-oh. Come along then", she said to Faustus as she clicked her fingers. Faustus felt himself being pulled by his shoulders, pulled forwards and then upwards. His soul was being dragged from his body. Lifted from the ground as if by two invisible hooks. One in each shoulder blade. He was lifted to six-foot, his spiritual toes stubbed the ground as he was dragged forward. His ghostly arms hung to his side like a deflated balloon animal. His hazy head flopped forwards, so all he could see was the floor. Lilith walked to the wall and pushed a brick. A door opened. The opening led to nothing but blackness. She just walked into the dark casually. Faustus had no interest in following, as he could feel the evil pushing from that darkness. And now, for the first time, he was afraid. He could feel the fear running through his - literal - spirit. He had no choice. The invisible strings of his puppet master dragged him forwards. Faustus vanished into the darkness. He managed to look back right at the end and saw his lifeless body on the ground. Once he had done so, the door swung shut, and the basement was once again silent.

### *Mary*

The birds sang and chirped in the mid-morning sunshine. The sun shone through the trees in the Institute courtyard. Lisa stood with her arm around Daniel's waist, Crystal and Martin on either side of them. "Do you think she is happy?" Lisa asked. A small vase with the name Mary Watkins engraved upon it sat under the tree. "I don't feel her now, so I hope so", Crystal said. "I wish we could have done more", she added as an afterthought. Daniel smiled. It was good to see her back to being slightly ditzy. He would be happy if he never saw the stern and commanding Crystal again. "But, was it ever really her?" Lisa asked. She took the question from Daniel's lips and spoke it aloud. Stolen like a teenage kiss in a playground, only Daniel was happy that he wasn't the one to ask. "I don't know", Crystal answered hesitantly. "You think it might have been Lilith all along? Lilith and her games?"

"But there was a body", Martin said and pointed at the vase. "We had it cremated!"

"Maybe it was both, maybe neither", Daniel said. "I don't think it matters". Lisa rubbed a tear from her eye. She hoped that nobody would notice, but Daniel did. "What's wrong?" He asked her. Lisa took a moment to reply. "I just think it's sad", she said. "This was a young woman, and nobody can find her parents? Nobody has come forward to claim her body? It feels so wrong, so pointless". They had all thought the same. This was a woman, little more than a girl, who had been kidnapped and then killed. Someone somewhere must have known her. Yet, nobody had come forward during the appeals, and nobody had spoken up. "Five years is a long time", Martin said. "Maybe they were immigrants and moved back home? Maybe she just had no family left?"

"I don't think we'll ever know", Crystal said. She looked at the vase and tried again to reach out. To touch something, but the vase was dead and empty. She was not sure how she felt about it. She had seen emptiness before after a soul had moved on. There was usually an echo left behind, a trace of what once was. She would have especially expected it in a traumatic death, but here there was nothing. In this case, though, maybe nothing was better than something, she thought to herself. Sometimes it is better to have nothing rather than have something that can cause you harm or will be troublesome. Maybe nothing was for the best in this case.

### *Daniel*

Daniel sat at home alone and looked at the piece of paper. He had told Lisa that he had gotten rid of it, and that had been true. Only the damn thing kept coming back.

The day after the *event*, he had binned it. It had been burning a hole in his pocket and rumbling the spaces in his mind. So he had got up early in the morning and thrown the thing into the black wheelie bin outside. Done, he had thought. The following day when he had gone downstairs, the page was sitting on his kitchen table.

He had thought about asking Lisa but then decided against it. He did not want to worry her, and it *was* just a trophy of sorts. It was a trophy that he did not want. He did not feel it was deserved either. *Had they won?* Not in his mind. David had died, as had other innocents, and for what, because a Deviless was bored? He had looked the page over, and it was still pristine. It should have been covered in bin juice and other nasties, but it was spotless. Thankfully, it was also blank. Daniel had then burnt it. He had sat in the kitchen over the sink and lit the bottom corner. The flames grew and then shrank no quicker or slower than he would have expected.

The soot and ash were washed down the sink's plughole, and that was that.

Until the following day.

It had been the most Monday of Mondays. The coffee had tasted stale, the weather had teetered between being somewhat okay and boringly miserable, and the power of motivation had taken a holiday. Daniel had pulled his jeans on and headed out into the world. He was shopping when he first felt it. A warmth in his pocket, a glow that radiated down his leg. Daniel thought nothing of it at first. He just presumed he'd caught his leg on something. Then, when he had reached the checkout and put his hand in his pocket, that was when he felt it. Smooth and folded in half, he could feel the smooth edges of the sheet. It was neatly folded and in his pocket. Daniel took his shopping and packed it. He then took the page from his pocket and looked it over. It was still blank, still perfect, and still - *it seemed* - his.

Daniel left the page on the side in the supermarket, not looking back as he left. A week passed, and the page seemed to be no more. Daniel would wake in the morning and check his pockets only to find them empty. When the letterbox clattered, he expected to see the page lying on his doormat, but it never happened. It would not be accurate to say that Daniel had forgotten about the page. *We do not forget things that quickly*. The page had, though, been stored in the back of his mind. The week had passed without incident, and by the following Monday, he had stopped jumping to check the mail when it arrived. It was Tuesday evening when it resurfaced. Daniel was heading upstairs to bed, it had been a solid day, and he had finished a fair amount of work. He had decided to lose himself in a book. It was his way to unwind, to unravel the coils of stress. He would travel to a mythical world under the lamplight and forget all about this world. Daniel opened the bedroom door, and then he saw it lying on his pillow. The page was back. This time it was different. There was creasing on the page. He could feel it in his gut, a grumbling groaning telling him that this time it was going to be strange, it was going to have a message. Daniel walked to the bed and picked up the page. He looked at it and read the message.

*"Daniel, I'm bored!"*

Printed in Great Britain
by Amazon